SISSY HUSBAND

1

A wife guides her femboy husband into feminization

Lady Alexa

Also by Lady Alexa

Becoming Joanne
Becoming Joanne 1
Becoming Joanne 2
Becoming Joanne 3

Femboy Love
Femboy Love 1

Feminized and Pretty
Feminized and Pretty 1
Feminized and Pretty 2
Feminized and Pretty 3
Feminized and Pretty 4

Forced Feminization
Forced Feminization Bundle 1

Subscribe to my blog charting my real-life FLR and forced feminisation lifestyle with my feminised husband Alice here:
www.ladyalexauk.com[1]
You can also subscribe to my newsletter and receive exclusive forced feminisation stories, news and offers by subscribing from my blog
www.ladyalexauk.com

Paul Paige has a deep secret from his wife, Gemma. He is a secret sissy femboy who visits professional ladies for a few hours of feminisation.

However, after he contacts Mistress Karlene who knows him from her past and befriends Gemma. Karlene tells Gemma about her husband's desires. After first being annoyed, Gemma sees the benefits of having a femboy husband, not least because of his failures in bed. Paul's future suddenly looks very different.

CONTENTS

Sissy Husband is an updated re-telling of an early two-book series called *A Sissy Cuckold Husband*.

The original was a classic forced feminisation story where a husband is feminised by a Mistress and his wife as a double act. They turn him into a submissive and cuckolded sissy.

I revisit my older books from time to time to update the covers and some of the inner text. While updating my *A Sissy Cuckold Husband* series, I noticed there was a slightly alternative storyline within the plot – that of a husband who visits professional mistresses to live out his sissy fantasy but keeps his dream a secret from his wife.

Once she finds out her husband's desires to be a femboy sissy through his former girlfriend who she befriends in the gym, she and her new friend set about realising his and their dream. Paul, the husband pushes back as he tackles his inner societal programming that being a sissy femboy is shameful.

The story now has more of a transgender awakening theme and of a mutually satisfying female-led relationship that satisfies everyone and is very different to what society considers the norm,

The original *Sissy Cuckold Husband* series is still available if you like the classic forced feminisation approach but I hope you enjoy my new twist on the story.

1 – Femboy Dream

He curtsied, holding out his short white dress. The seated lady wore a tight black leather dress with her black hair pulled back in a tight high ponytail. A smirk faded from her lips. "Kiss my feet, sissy boy."

Paul Paige scuttled to her and knelt. The feeling of the tiny dress around the top of his smooth bare thighs and her firm instruction caused his penis to slam against his flat silicone chastity cage. He bent to kiss the toes of Mistress Alana's black high-heeled shoes.

"Good sissy boy," said Mistress Alana. "You are a pretty femboy, aren't you?"

"Yes, Mistress," he replied, his mouth dry with the excitement of his situation. Kneeling before this powerful lady wearing a light dress, his hair tied in two side ponytails and held in with two large pink ribbons.

"Stand." Mistress Alana lifted her hand in a lifting motion.

He stood his face to the floor, his penis fighting against its cage and losing.

"Lift your dress front, sissy boy."

He lifted the front of his dress and his head went light with the exhilaration of the moment. Mistress had not allowed him to wear panties and she stared with contempt at his penis locked in a flat silicone cage in the shape of a female vagina. A small ring was attached around his balls.

Mistress Alana lifted his smooth balls with two fingertips. "My, these are cute and girly. Your clitty is so small, it fits nicely in the flat vagina cage. I've seen real women with bigger clitties than your little thing." She looked up at him, her hand still under his balls. She squeezed. He gasped in ecstasy and desire. "Tell me you want to be a girl, 'cause I know you do."

At that moment, he wanted nothing more. "Yes, Mistress, I want to be a girl."

"And how much do you want to be girl, sissy boy?"

He was breathing rapidly. "Yes, very much, Mistress."

"Very much is enough. Tell me how much you want to be a girl. How you want me to turn you into a real girl with real tits and a cute round bottom. Tell me sissy boy."

"Yes Mistress, I am desperate for you to turn me into a real girl. Please do that, please."

Mistress Alana glanced at her watch. She dropped his balls and stood up. "That's it for tonight, sissy boy, time's up." She took a key and unlocked his cage. It fell into her hand and she passed it to him with disinterest. She got up and wandered to a side table, picked up her phone and started to scroll through it. "Get changed and leave my 900 cash on the seat, there's a good boy."

Paul deflated with disappointment. He'd have to pay for more next time. Three hours was nowhere near enough. As he changed into his business suit and shook out the ponytails, he thought about the evening. The usual story for his wife. "Sorry Gemma, the meeting overran." He'd then try to make love to her with the memories of what Mistress Alana did for him. What he really wanted more than anything was to put on a pretty dress when he got home or a cute tennis skirt. Pinks and whites. Yellow maybe.

Sure, Gemma was stunningly beautiful and assertive in her own way. But there was no way he'd admit to his wife what he really wanted. He explained his smooth body as his gym body. No way he'd say it was to feel feminine. He'd find a new Mistress to replace Alana. Mistress Alana was good but the sudden switch from focussed domme to a distant business-only disinterest left him frustrated. Especially at 300 an hour. Not that he couldn't afford that, it was small change.

Yes, he'd find someone new. Someone who loved femboy sissies for being femboy sissies, not for a business relationship.

He left the wad of large 100-value bills behind and left Mistress Alana's apartment. He took the stairs two flights down and left the front door to the block just as a man in an expensive business suit took the door before it closed. Mistress Alana's next client.

Paul stood on the pavement and called John Smart, his Finance Director. It rang once and picked up. "Hi, Paul. What's up."

Paul Paige shared a secret with his Finance guy. They once went for a few drinks and one thing led to another and they found they were both secret femboys. "John. I need a favour. My current lady is treating me like a business transaction. I need someone better. Someone caring. Someone who loves, well you know, men like us. Any suggestions?"

"Well," John replied. "Maybe."

"Go on."

"I have never used her, but I've heard about her through the grapevine."

"And?"

"She's not cheap."

"The best never is."

"I don't have her number but I know someone who knows someone who said this lady is everything you're looking for. I'll send you her number once I've made a call."

A smile crept over Paul's face. He needed an outlet for his needs and desires. He was rich. So what if she was pricey. He had to pay, he could hardly tell Gemma he wanted to wear skimpy little dresses and skirts, have a pretty hairstyle and be a maid or servant. No, he was the CEO of his own company. How could he, Paul Paige, become a girly femboy who wore little girl clothes and worked as a maid? It's why he had to pay. Part-time submissive femboy was his lot in life. Part-time was better than not at all."

He waved at a taxi and it pulled over and he clambered in. He gave the driver his home address. Ten minutes later, his phone pinged. It was John. The message only gave a number and name. Mistress Karlene.

Paul's chest thumped as his heart beat faster. He pressed the number on his phone screen and put the phone to his ear.

2– Dominant

Karlene Adair was a dominatrix. She was not any run-of-the-mill dominatrix; men couldn't find her services in the personals or those annoying pop-ups on fetish websites sites. Her service was exclusive and word of mouth.

Karlene was slim, tall, intelligent and beautiful. She could have been anything she wanted: a supermodel, an A-list film star, an academic or a celebrity therapist. She chose to be a discrete mistress to those who could pay. They were men who projected a veneer of heterosexual masculinity but had deep secrets inside them; behind closed doors, they secretly preferred to be compliant feminine sissies.

Her single purpose was to turn these wealthy men into her submissive sissy girls. Mistress Karlene loved and excelled at her work. Males flocked to her for a few hours of feminine and submissive relief before donning their manly disguises once again.

The sissy cowering at her feet at that moment was one such man. But Karlene had a problem; this was becoming too easy. She liked to push against boundaries. What she wanted was to find a man who she could guide to live fully as a sissy. A man she could help to become the girl he truly desired to be, not a three-hour evening release.

But where were those challenges? She'd transformed this outwardly assertive male at her feet into a weeping sissy. It was too easy and in an hour, he'd be back in his expensive business suit pretending to be an alpha male in a boardroom somewhere while dreaming of his time with her.

Karlene twisted her long slim fingers before her client's adoring eyes. She preferred the term client, this was after all, a professional relationship. That said, she adored being with femboys. She hated alpha men, they were so full of fake machismo. No, give her a femboy any day. Not for sex, no. For something else, a kind of power kick? She wasn't entirely sure but that didn't matter, there were plenty of hunks to use for sex. The femboys received their feminisation and punishment, she received their money and a whole lot of pleasure from her power kick.

Karlene's nails were long and red; the talons of a professional predator. She scratched them over the shivering head of this supposedly powerful male at her feet. He was currently a docile sissy. She had removed his body hair; his arms, legs and chest were as smooth as a young girl's. What would he tell his wife? She didn't care.

Her sissy wore a frilly little girl's party dress with *Little Princess* on the front and frilly panties. She loved to put them in little girl's clothes. His panties showed under the dress; it was too short to cover them. Their dresses always were, she preferred that. It added to their vulnerability and she liked male vulnerability. Sometimes it might be pink ballerina skirts, other times schoolgirl skirts and blouses. Her favourite was the princess dress; she saved that one for special occasions.

She loved to see white frilly ankle socks on a sissy's large feet, followed by cute white shoes with a single buckle. She used an online store for outsized little girls' shoes. She pulled his hair into two small sissy pigtails on the side of his head using pink bows.

Karlene sighed, this was what life was all about. Proving that macho males were sissy girls. Her lithe fingers played with his little dick through his panties. It was as hard as a rod. A small rod.

Sissy's face had a pained look of ecstasy. She loved the humiliation showing in his eyes. She wrapped a hand around his shaved balls through the panties. Sissy gasped, panting, breathless. They all loved her controlling little clitties. She liked controlling sissy clitties too. She squeezed her fingers on his balls and he squealed like a baby piglet. She never squeezed too hard but enough to make their eyes water. Was he crying? She hoped so. Crying with the love and the pain.

She dug her fingers inside his panties and scratched her fingernails up and down his little erection. It was obvious he was desperate to cum. She stopped, she didn't want sissy mess, oh no. Yuk. She gazed into his tearful desperate eyes; eyes full of intense desire and love for her. Her face was inches away, her lips parted, her breath on his. She knew he wanted to kiss her, to feel her tongue. That was never going to happen.

He calmed down, his need to cum receded. She pulled his panties to his ankles and circled a forefinger over the end of his erection, bringing him to the brink of orgasm again. She stopped. This was such good fun. He wept in his desperation to cum, he pleaded with her, "Please Mistress Karlene, please let me cum. Please."

A drop of pre-cum sissy juice oozed from the end of his little erection. She let the bead of pre-cum drop onto the end of her finger. She waved it back and forth in front of his eyes. It hypnotised him. She pushed his mouth open with a forefinger of each hand. "Open your mouth, sissy, and put out your tongue."

He pushed out his tongue with a look of fear. She wiped the end of her cum-covered finger onto the end of his tongue. She closed his mouth and held his nose, making him swallow. He shuddered but his eyes said thank you.

"Training for when you taste the cum of other femboys like you." She loved nothing more than to have two sissies and make them play together. "Or maybe real men? Let's see." She knew several men who liked easy transgendered girls. Especially when they were part-time sissies.

She trained her sissies until they were obsequious, subservient little girls. Just as they wanted. Someone to take away their shame at what they really wanted in life. She was their excuse – *She made me do it, I didn't want to become a sissy femboy, I had no choice* – that's what they told themselves.

Then it was the time to take them to play with her experienced sissies. This sissy at her feet wasn't ready yet. Making her sissies play together was the biggest fun of all. She loved to guide her new sissy's erect cocks into the open waiting mouths of her experienced sissies. The first time was the best, the look of distaste as another sissy put lips around their precious little cockettes: priceless. She would then turn them around and guided their hard cockettes into her new pansy-girl's tight firm sissy vagina.

Then they would go back to their big business offices, They'd make love to their wives in the evenings dreaming she was a sissy.

She needed new challenges though. A new idea had come to her. She would add a sideline: A mistress tutor. She'd teach wives and mistresses how to make their husbands and clients into submissive sissy femboys.

For now, she needed this new sissy well-trained and ready for sissy love. She went back to work on his erection, playing, taunting, bringing him to the brink then letting him down.

Then she'd lock him up in a tight cage and tickle his little clitty through the bars. He'd drizzle out. Another ruined orgasm, how delightful.

3 – It's business

Karlene Adair entered the Coffee Bean Café, an upmarket coffee bar in the business area. Even Mistresses to the rich and famous needed a break. It was early afternoon and a soft murmur of voices bubbled over low background jazz music. She sat at a circular marble-topped table next to a plate glass window looking out onto the street. The backwards words *Coffee Bean* were etched in large brown writing on the glass. The image of a roasted bean replaced the *'a'* in Bean.

A sign over the marble counter said, *bar service*. She called to a young man cleaning the tables. He came over, a cloth in one hand, a name tag on his chest announcing him as Wayne.

"Wayne dear, bring me a small Americano, a shot of skimmed milk, no sugar. There's a good boy."

"I'm awfully sorry, Madam," Wayne said. "But the Coffee Bean is counter service."

"Yes, Wayne, I know that." She glared. "Just get it, would you? Off you go."

He scampered away and returned with her drink. Mistress Karlene acknowledged him with a small nod. The boy waited, his eyes falling over her long legs and large breasts.

"Go." Karlene waved him away with a flick of her fingers.

Wayne hadn't cleared her table yet and a free local newspaper lay open across the surface. She was about to call Wayne back when a large colour photo caught her attention. She picked it up, holding the pages open double-width. Karlene recognised the man in the photo.

He was a little grey around the temples these days; it suited him. He was wearing a dark blue suit that screamed expensive and made-to-measure. His dark-brown hair was long, over his ears and collar. He had filled out. Not fat, but the weight that comes with maturity and gym work. And success. He grinned into the camera with a look of confidence and power. The headline stated:

LOCAL ENTREPRENEUR OPENS NEW BUSINESS HQ IN CITY

There was no doubt who the local entrepreneur was: Paul Paige, from her college days. Or as she had called him back then: *Pansy Princess*. He had been her first, the starting pistol on her race to transform wealthy men into sissies.

A small smile spread across her wide sensual lips, a hint of perfect white teeth peeked through. She still thought of him as *Pansy Princess*. At five foot six, he was four inches shorter than her. That was before she put heels on.

Who would have guessed Paul Paige had a strong female side from this newspaper photo? Beneath the expensive suit and assertive smile, Karlene knew this successful businessman had a small dick and wore feminine underwear. Pretty dresses in private. Or used to. She'd introduced him to wearing panties, bras and little dresses back in those sepia-coloured college days.

How many men compensated for lack of size and a hidden female side through over-achievement and fake machismo? Karlene knew that answer well enough. Well, well, how long had it been? Ten years? They had been students together, twenty-one years old and about to start out in life. The warm memories of Pansy Princess in their final semesters at college ran through her mind. They had met in their MBA classes and dated for the final two semesters. They both graduated with distinction and went their separate ways.

Dated may not have been the correct word if she was being exact. She didn't allow him to have penetrative sex with her; his dick was far too small for that. They went out some time but as soon as they came back to her room, she put him in pretty clothes and made him serve her and lick her out. She'd play with his little dick but never let him cum when they were together. Sissy cum was disgusting anyway.

There were plenty of college boys with big dicks she'd had sex with. But she'd only wanted them for sex. Pansy Paul was the person she preferred to spend time with, even when she was sucking on someone else's dick or riding him. Paul used to be devastated seeing her taking other men but loved it once she'd had her way and threw them out and cuddled him. He was the one even if he wasn't allowed to have sex with her. There was more to a relationship than physical sex.

Paul had been serious and business-like. And conservative. She had spotted something else in him, something feminine, sissy, girly. She brought out his latent femboy tendencies. It hadn't been too hard. She wondered if anyone else had found his sissy side since then. Did he pay for mistresses? She guessed he did. Once a man had tasted sissiness, there was no going back. Did he date men dressed as a girl? She'd not guided him that far but it was there. It was a possibility. Males loved to be treated as sissy girls.

Karlene sat back on her chair, a flume of thin steam rose from her dark coffee. Who would have thought? *Pansy Princess*. Spits of rain hit against the plate-glass café window, brown leaves swirled in a mini-tornado thrown up by gusts of wind. People pushed by along the damp concrete footpath, heads down, oblivious to anything in their focus to get home. Cars nudged forward nose to tail, windscreen wipers flapping and brake lights flashing red.

A smile spread across her long luscious mouth. She licked the bottom of her lip, like a Persian cat about to devour fresh cream. *Pansy* would be her fresh cream again. Fate had played its hand. Here was a ready pansy served up on a plate for her.

She liked them wealthy and small down below, like Pansy Princess. It made things so much easier when they had tiny cockettes and little Pansy Princess had the tiniest dick she had ever seen. Before or since. She grinned at the memory. He had more of a clitty than a dick. As she used to remind him constantly. How she loved to see his embarrassed face. She knew he liked it too because it got so hard when she giggled at it and told him how ridiculous it was.

It had been pure chance she'd gone into the Coffee Bean that afternoon. It was destiny spotting Pansy Princess's happy and unaware face as it peered at her from a free newspaper discarded by a busy customer.

She read the article with relish. He had opened his new company headquarters as his business was expanding. The article said he headed a $50M turnover business called Cochin Inc. growing at 20% a year. She sat up, she smelled money and a whole lot of fun. A flurry of excitement surged in her chest. She recognised the feeling. She had it every time she started the hunt.

The article said he was married. This was not unexpected, despite being on the short side he was a good-looking man. A pretty boy. And he was now wealthy. A wife was never an obstacle to sissifying any male; Karlene had yet to meet any wife who could match her in looks, confidence and sexual allure. The wife would be an element of guilt for Pansy for the few moments before Karlene's allure entranced him as it did for all sissies. She wondered if he went home and changed into a sissy for his wife. She doubted it, they rarely did.

Her phone rang. "Hello?" she said in her deep assertive style.

Silence.

"Hello."

"Er, hello. Er, is that Mistress Karlene?"

"Yes."

Silence for several seconds. She let the male caller stew. The voice was vaguely familiar. "I was given your number by a business colleague. He said you're the best in your line of work."

"Best at what may I ask?" She taunted him, making the caller squirm at having to say what he wanted.

"The best at being a, a, a Mistress."

"I am. What exactly are you looking for? Feminisation? Sissification? Female Domination?" She spoke in normal volume and the couple on the adjoining table looked up with a start. She had nothing to be ashamed of. She and her clients were consenting adults.

Silence for a moment. "Yes, all of that."

"1,000 an hour. I can come to your place or you can come to mine." Word of mouth. It always worked.

"OK. You can come to my office, 298, Durham Avenue. Cochin Inc. HQ. 7pm. This evening, everyone will be leaving. I'll leave word with my receptionist."

"And who shall I ask for?"

"Say you're an investor and you have an appointment with Mr Paige. Paul Paige."

Karlene nearly dropped the phone. She composed herself. "7pm."

She searched for Cochin Inc. on her phone browser. The new headquarters address came up. It was ten walk minutes from where she was, in the heart of the business district. Perfect.

The article said Paul Paige was holding a board meeting there this afternoon. She got up and moved across the Coffee Bean like a falcon gliding on a thermal, searching for prey. For the first time in a long time, a tingle of nerves hit her. Paul Paige, Pansy Princess. This was fate. So. His wife didn't know his proclivity for being feminised or he wouldn't be looking to pay 1,000 an hour for her services. How wonderful. Maybe his wife could be the first client for her new idea – teaching wives to feminise their men.

Her long metal earrings jangled as she strode with natural assured confidence. Four-inch spike heels clicked like a time bomb against the tiled floor. Male customers glanced up to follow her swivelling bottom. Her legs extended forever from her short dress. Her thick dark hair flayed around her bare light brown-skinned shoulders and down to her waist. It flowed down her back like windswept ocean waves lapping against the coast. She spotted the male onlookers from her peripheral vision, the salivating male masses. They all came under her sensuous erotic spell. And they were all girly sissies inside if only they took the time to accept it.

Mistress Karlene Adair: intelligent, beautiful with a panther-like sensuality. A panther on the prowl. She narrowed her eyes; she was a heartbreaker, a vixen and a ball-breaking dominatrix. And Pansy Princess with the tiny cockette was in her sights again. But now, maybe his wife too.

4 – Temptation

Karlene sat cool and controlled, her back as straight as a board. She perched on the edge of a black leather chair in the soulless reception area of Cochin Inc. Karlene checked the time on her watch, 7.11pm. Late. Pansy would pay for that. Another 500 plus a spanking. He'd love that, financial domination plus spanked like a naughty girl.

She shook back her mane of long swirling brown hair. It flicked around her waist and over her massive round boobs. A little silicone assistance did no harm whatsoever.

The young fair-haired receptionist wore a dark-blue corporate jacket sat behind a tall wooden desk. She kept looking up at Karlene with eyes that said, *You are not an investor, at least not in the business sense.* Behind her, Cochin Inc. was written in 18-inch metal letters against a backdrop of modern city skyscrapers.

"Mr Paige is coming out to meet you now. His board meeting has just finished," the receptionist said as if announcing the next train at a station.

A double door to the side sprung open. Several men and women in dark suits burst through, foreheads creased in discussion, some holding folders. They passed her, heading to the lifts. The eyes of each man fell over Karlene as they walked by. Paul Paige followed last, his face alive with a broad smile, his arms wide. His face then dropped like a stone. He recognised Karlene instantly and froze as he put two and two together.

Karlene smiled at him sweetly, appraising and analysing him. She had the experience she never had at college. She was starting out then. Things were going to be different this time.

"Er, Karlene. I er, didn't, Er. This is a shock. Er. So good to see you again." He stood back to take her in, shock etched in his eyes, his mouth hanging open. His suit looked expensive and his shirt tie-less and thick with quality. He stood erect as if to make up for his lack of height. "Ten years. I didn't expect you'd be *that* Karlene." He was recovering his composure with the assured manner of a business leader. He looked at her over again. "How are you? How did you get into this, er, business?"

"So many questions, darling." She pouted.

Paul Paige's face flashed red. She smiled, tilted her head and he relaxed.

She didn't think of him as Paul Paige the businessman but Pansy Princess. He was even more formal and reserved than she remembered him as a student. She would change that, she wanted to see him as Pansy again. As soon as possible. She shivered at the thought.

He looked her over and down her body, settling a moment too long on the tops of her large breasts, tight and exposed by a low-cut top. His 5ft 6ins height put them at his eye-level with her, she stood 6ft 1in in four-inch heels. Male lust, it was there with all of them, even little Pansy. He may be a big important businessman nowadays, but he would always be Pansy to her.

"It's nice to see you again," she said, biting back the words *Pansy* and *Princess*. She didn't want to humiliate him in front of his receptionist. No, she still cared for him, she'd wait a while before humiliating him once again. Karlene balled her hands tight at the prospect. Her move to the new city was paying dividends on the first day. Pansy Princess had called her. A warm glow flowed through her chest. This was far better than she would ever have dreamed.

He put an arm on her bare back, her short mini dress was cut away behind from the neck to the small of her back. His eyes settled on the top of the round bottom. She never allowed sissies to touch her. For Pansy, she made an exception. He was small in height and small in dick, but he had personality and she liked that. A pansy personality.

"Come with me, Karlene, let's go to my private room. We can catch up on the past ten years." He looked at his watch. She could see his nervousness beneath the confident smooth exterior. "In the circumstances, we'll forget the reason for my call and just talk."

"Sure," she said, her smile broadening, her pout increasing. Men liked to play the big important man.

Paul turned towards the receptionist. "You can leave now, Vicky, everyone else has left for the evening."

The receptionist stood and thanked him, her eyes running over Karlene. She grabbed a bag and coat from under the desk and headed for the lifts. Karlene followed Paul through the door. There was no question, he would be desperate to be a sissy again despite what he'd said.

He had filled out a little since college days, as hinted from his newspaper photo, but he was still slim. He looked defined, as if he'd been busy in the gym. He used to be skinny, the way she preferred her men. She would take him back to being slimmer; muscles had no place on femboys in her world. Sissies needed to be demure and feminine.

He showed her through the deserted offices, past a desk next to a large black door. Paul Paige, CEO Cochin Inc. was written on the door in large silver letters. He had succeeded, as he had planned. Karlene knew beneath all his business leader bravado, he was still Pansy. He was a femboy who paid for mistresses to feminise him. His phone call proved that.

They entered his large office, set in the corner of the fourteenth floor. Floor-to-ceiling windows lined two sides of the room. A cream leather sofa was along one glass wall and an oval mahogany meeting table with six chairs sat in the middle of the room.

Paul went to the sofa and sat. He ushered her to follow him, playing the big man. Karlene sat next to him and let her bare leg brush against his and her short skirt to ride up her thigh. She pressed her leg more firmly against his leg and leaned into him. His musky aftershave was strong and masculine. She would change that to something sweeter and more feminine.

Panic shot over his face feeling her leg against his. He tried to revert to macho mode. She had him rattled, her beauty and close attention on him was having the effect she expected. She had been in offices and rooms like this many times before, with powerful businessmen, politicians and TV stars. All of them over-compensated for their tiny cocks and stature with fake macho bravado. She had broken them all into demure little sissy girls, emasculated into becoming femboy princesses.

They paid her a lot for the privilege of being emasculated. It was certainly a privilege for them to spend time in the presence of Mistress Karlene Adair. Mistress to femboy sissies. It was what life was for.

Karlene's eyes followed Paul's lips as he described his work. She nodded at the right places and smiled when he did. She wasn't listening to his words merely his emphasis. Every so often she placed a long slim hand on his thigh and left it there for a few moments. She crossed her legs and her small dress rode up further, exposing the tops of slender light brown bare thighs. His eyes darted to them as he spoke. She let a single shoe dangle from a toe. His eyes widened.

"You've done so well, Paulie." Karlene's voice was soft, demure and breathless. "I can't believe we were so young back then in college."

Paul was different to the others, she liked him a lot at college. She made him girly once they were alone and he was himself finally: a sissy femboy. He still had something sweet about him. She would convert him into her pansy femboy again, of course, but she would be caring and thoughtful. Loving. After all, it was what he wanted at heart. He'd called her for that very purpose after all.

Karlene shuffled up closer to him and leant into his face, her lips close to his ear. She placed her hand on his thigh and kept it there. She looked into his eyes, tilting her head, giving him time to take in her expensive perfume. Her tight dress rode up further, exposing a hint of tiny white panties. Her hair tumbled over her face; thick, brown and shining.

"You look like you keep fit, Paulie," Karlene said, as she ran a long fine hand down along his arm, squeezing his bicep. She wanted to say Pansy but had to be subtle. For now.

Karlene hummed and her fingers danced down his arm, past his hand and onto the side of his hips. Paul glanced towards the door, his eyes wide in panic as if he expected to see someone outside. He was sweating and he placed a finger inside his shirt collar and ran it around his neck. "Karlene. I said to forget what I said on the call. It's nice to meet up again. Nothing more. I'll find someone else."

She smiled again, a wide smirk. She had him on the back foot. He would not be able to resist her, they never could. Her dominant allure. It was time to move in. "Do you remember our time together at college, Paulie?"

She saw his memories flooding back. Her eyes widened in fake innocence. "Let's forget about that. Let's just reminisce."

She ignored him. "Do you remember what I used to call you?"

He squirmed on the sofa. His face creased up, his eyes like slits. She could see he remembered.

"I called you Pansy Princess." Karlene's hand moved closer to his crotch. "And I remember your cock was so small, like a girl's clitty. And I called you Pansy because." She looked to the ceiling in thought. "Because you were so feminine."

He cringed in horror. "Karlene." His voice trembled.

"Do you remember that?" She stared at him. "Pansy?"

Karlene's voice was soft, kind. Bestowing the name *Pansy Princess* on him was an act of kindness, something honourable for her to do for him. He loved it and it made him swoon. It was having the same effect this evening.

Her little finger twitched over his fly zipper. His face flushed, he breathed in and held his breath. She placed a second finger there, rubbing softly over his trouser fly. She thought she felt his erection under the zipper. It wasn't obvious; his penis was so small.

"Do you remember you used to sob like a little girl when I played with your little clitty but didn't let you cum?"

Karlene's voice remained gentle, teasing but loving. He said, "*Yes,*" his voice was a distant dry croak, his throat caught.

"Do you remember when I'd blow on your little clitty? I'd tease you but never put it in my mouth? And you'd cry and plead like the sissy boy you are. Pansy Princess. Her hand moved over his flies and she pushed her palm into his erection. "I want you to be Pansy Princess again for me. My sissy femboy. But this time I know so much more and have so much experience. We can go a lot further, as far as you want. Maybe you've been with other sissies, maybe men too."

"Karlene," he said through dry lips. "I'm married."

Karlene kneaded his erection through his trousers. He hadn't pushed her away. She hooked the zipper between two fingertips and slid it down. Paul watched her fingers, a sigh of pleasure escaped, but his face showed turmoil.

Karlene registered his comment about being married; her smile continued without a break.

"I loved and cared for you, Pansy. Do you remember? I'll be loving and caring to you again, my pretty princess."

A resolve swept across his face and he sat up and went to move away, "Yes, I remember Karlene and it was ten years ago. A lot has changed since then. We're no longer young students, we're thirty-five years old. And I'm happily married. Maybe I pay for Mistresses to feminise me as a release valve. But it means nothing and Gemma doesn't know."

Karlene slid her little finger inside the open fly and touched his penis through his underpants. He was rock-hard. She wasn't surprised, she never failed, it's how she controlled all her sissies and how she would make him into Pansy again. "Don't worry about Gemma, Pansy, we should tell her and include her in everything." Two for the price of one.

She raised her other hand and stroked his face. Her lips moved closer to his, brushing the side of his mouth. Her hand slipped inside his trouser fly, her hands fondled him through the striped cotton boxers. He froze; she saw he was torn. It was time to make the next move. This was just like old times.

He would be Pansy Princess again.

5 – Rejection

She flipped Paul's boxer shorts open at the front. His little cockette poked out hard and proud, upright like a tiny stick, lost among the folds of soft underwear. It was so cute, so girly; she felt a catch in her throat, this is what she lived for. This man, outwardly proud and confident, was reduced to a frozen sissy with a tiny hard cockette.

She looked into his conflicted eyes and brushed his cheek with her lips. He froze, unable to move as her hand meandered over his face, the other on his little cockette. His eyes swivelled to the door again as Karlene put a thumb and forefinger on the end of his little cock. She rubbed the foreskin down and back up. Her light touch was expert and gentle. Her other hand rubbed his ear and then across to his lips. She parted his lips and pushed in to touch his tongue with her thumb

Paul's eyes glazed, as if he were in a spell. He groaned, his body stiffened. His eyes opened and for a moment he looked angry. He pulled away from Karlene, his face flushed red, his breathing fast, his mouth set tight. "What are you doing, Karlene?" He gasped and looked away from her. "We're not at college any more." His face was bright red. "I didn't realise it was you when I called. This isn't going to happen."

Karlene kept her thumb and forefinger on the end of his little penis. "What's the problem, Pansy Princess?"

"I told you, Karlene, I'm married. I have a beautiful wife. Gemma."

He hadn't pushed her hand away and she rubbed gently on his erection.

"Gemma's a supermodel. I can't get back with you as a previous girlfriend. It's wrong." His words tumbled out like boulders rolling down a hill. "I adore her. We married three years ago. We're in love. Sorry, Karlene. I can't do this. It's wonderful, you're wonderful. In any other circumstances, I would fall for you again. But it's wrong. I can't. I don't do the pansy thing any more with you. It was just a game and we were young. Now I need dispassionate Mistresses for a short game that hurts no one."

He picked up his phone and flicked through photos as Karlene stroked his penis. He chose one and pushed an image of a tall blond beautiful lady into her face. His flies were open and his tiny erection firm in excitement. Karlene's fingers worked at his foreskin with gentle, light touches as she glanced seductively at the image. He still hadn't pushed her away.

His face was a mix of relief and pride at his wife. Karlene dropped his little cock. It stood up, like a tiny spring bud. She sat straight, looked at the screen and put a hand around the phone.

"She's pretty, Pansy, but there's no need to worry, this can be our secret. I've never told anyone you're a sissy femboy. Gemma need never know."

Paul cleared his throat. "Gemma and I have a traditional marriage and sex is great. We are loyal and we respect each other completely. There are no problems of any kind in our relationship. It's perfect and I don't want to do anything to ruin what we have. I appreciate the offer, I do, but I can't do this. I see Mistresses from time to time to satisfy my needs but she doesn't know. I don't think she'd like to know my interest in this area."

"These are excuses, Princess," Karlene said.

He stood and poked his little cock away and zipped up his fly. He made to go to the door. Karlene put on an exaggerated look of disappointment.

"I'll be seeing *little clitty* again soon, Princess, you can count on it. I know you want to be Pansy Princess again. This time for good. You should come out into the open as Pansy Princess, it's what you want and I'm certain that if Gemma loves you, she'd understand and embrace the real you."

He looked away in embarrassment. "We have guests coming tonight. Gemma and I. At our home." He glanced at his watch to emphasise the point. "I need to go."

A small grin reappeared on her lips. That wasn't true. He'd phoned her expecting a session as a sissy boy. She licked her lips. "That's OK, sweetie, I understand." She crossed one leg over the other and sat back. "Don't worry, I can finish what I started when you have more time, my Pansy. I know you want to be a femboy and I know you want to be my femboy."

Karlene stood and walked to him. She saw his eyes flow over her breasts, her dusky fleshy mounds were large and firm. His body stiffened, his face went wary as she moved in close and ran a hand over his face cheek and down his arm. Her fingers ran down his side and to his bottom. She touched his bottom cheek and pulled him close.

"You, Pansy, are my little princess." Her voice was firm. "I have lots of sissy boys to play with." She fixed his eyes with hers and put her lush wide lips to one of his ears. "But you, Pansy Princess, were always my favourite. The first and the special one."

She allowed the hint of a grin. She shook her mane of thick dark hair back and her earrings jingled like tiny bells. Karlene moved away, allowing him to head for the door again. He wiped his forehead with the back of a hand.

"Pansy?" she said.

He turned back to face her, his hands on the door handle, his eyes darting with nerves waiting for her to speak.

Karlene put her head to one side and said in a voice tinged with syrup. "Pansy Princess, it's inevitable. I know you want to be my princess too. And Gemma's."

He pointed to the door. "Time to leave, Karlene." Karlene shrugged her shoulders and smirked. Not only would she make him into Pansy Princess again, but this time she would go a whole lot further than she had gone before. She'd guide him to his destiny with his wife.

Karlene held her hands together in excitement. This was such good fun; this was the challenge she had sought.

6 – Training

The buzzer sounded on Karlene's intercom two days later. It was 2 pm sharp; Paul Paige's wife, Gemma, was dead on time. Karlene liked punctuality, it showed a firm and confident personality. Karlene clicked her fingers at a small slim maid standing waiting by the door. The maid scampered to the entry pad. A small screen by the door showed Gemma waiting below. The pretty maid buzzed her in and, from her seat, Karlene saw Gemma enter the foyer.

The maid was small with a blond bob hairstyle with a pink bow in her hair. She wore a bright pink housemaid's dress that flared out with layers of white petticoats. She curtsied to Karlene and waited by the door. The maid kept her eyes on the floor. She wore a small white apron over the dress.

Gemma heard the lift whirring up to her top-floor city-centre penthouse apartment. "Open the door, Candy," she ordered. Candy opened the door and waited for the guest.

Karlene had a sixth sense about Gemma and her senses rarely let her down. Her senses told her there was a dormant dominant goddess inside Gemma. She would not be with Pansy Paul if she didn't have a dominant side. It's what he craved. The goddess needed awakening. She'd be Goddess Gemma. It sounded good and her first client as a Mistress tutor although Gemma didn't know that yet.

In truth, domination was there in most women. Pansy Paul was submissive below his false alpha facade. He was in love with his wife and this meant there was something strong inside her. She probably didn't think about his feminine side, wives rarely did. Once she had shown Gemma the promised land, she would want it. Karlene was certain of that.

Karlene had called Paul the morning after their encounter at his office. She'd explained she wanted to get to know his wife if they were to rekindle their friendship. Karlene had told him how wanted to find female friends. She added that Gemma must be a wonderful lady if he was so much in love with her so she would love to be friends with his lovely lady too.

Karlene knew Paul was relieved she had seemingly changed her attitude to him. He arranged for Gemma and Karlene to meet. Karlene smiled at the thought, Pansy Paul always did as he was told by strong confident women. She guessed Gemma got her own way often. The sub-domme relationship was probably already there if you looked.

Two days after Karlene's encounter with Paul at his office, she would be meeting his beautiful wife. She would show Gemma how to turn her powerful businessman husband into the sweet little girly femboy he so desired. She would put him in girl's party dresses, cheerleader outfits and schoolgirl uniforms just as she had done ten years ago. Gemma will love the power and the fun and Paul will love being himself once again. And she'd show Gemma how to find a real man with a proper cock.

She would add cuckolding to the mix just as she'd done ten years ago, Pansy also enjoyed that even though he complained. His complaints were part of the game, and it was a game. Gemma must be frustrated with Paul's little dick. She was tall and beautiful and must have had big cocks before meeting Pansy. Karlene guessed she missed that. It wouldn't take much. A little nudge and Pansy would be a cuckold again and Gemma satisfied. Both would get what they wanted. And Karlene would bask in her power.

Karlene rubbed her hands together. She loved a challenge. Cuckolding and making him Gemma's sissy would be an act of love. A gift from her to Gemma. Paul's evident love for Gemma would be the key as he will want to please her.

Karlene had let Gemma believe they would be having a friendly chat over coffee at her home. It was true Karlene wanted a female friend, but it was to share her vocation in life. A Mistress is fun but can be lonely with only sissies for company. Besides, Gemma looked hot and Karlene planned to have a little fun along the way.

Karlene had invited Gemma to seduce her into becoming a heartbreaking, cuckolding Goddess wife and to share their love of being dominant. How hot would that be for Gemma to cuckold her husband with a woman?

Karlene was also going to demonstrate the benefits of having a well-hung, sexy, powerful boyfriend purely for sex and to have Pansy Paul as her submissive cuckold sissy princess. Once Gemma experienced an eleven-inch rock-hard cock inside her, there would be no going back and Paul's days using his little maggot-like penis would be over. What is there not to love about that scenario? And Karlene would be in the middle of everything.

Gemma was going to experience a new world of love, affection and power. Karlene could not contain her excitement at the prospects of her plan. She tapped the floor with a foot, waiting for it to begin.

Karlene heard footsteps echo in the marbled passageway outside her door. Gemma appeared in the doorway, a sweet open smile lit her round fair-skinned face. A look of innocence and naivety flickered in her eyes. Good. Candy curtsied and Gemma threw her a look of total bewilderment.

Gemma was as tall as her and wore a mid-thigh white dress with shoulder straps highlighting her muscled shoulders. She wore matching white glossy high-heeled shoes. Her blond hair had a styled windswept look. She looked as if she had just stepped off the cover of a fashion magazine.

Karlene got up and strode to the entrance. Gemma walked towards her, eyes trailing on Candy. She walked with one foot in front of the other as if on an invisible tightrope. Karlene noted her calm and assured manner. And beauty. Gemma took Karlene's fingers, shook her hand and kissed her on one cheek. "Lovely to meet you, Gemma," said Karlene.

"Likewise," said Gemma. Gemma wore sheer light tan stockings that glistened on her slim, well-defined legs. Long model's legs. Her dress was fifties style and flared out from a small waist with white polka dots. The top of her dress held her large round breasts in tightly. They spilled out from a low-cut front, in much the same way as Karlene's. Pansy Paul liked big boobs, that was clear. She could work with that trait. A weakness many males shared. Maybe she would give him big boobs too? Now there's an idea.

Gemma smiled and her teeth glinted as if she were in a toothpaste commercial. Her enormous round blue eyes sparkled like two searchlights flashing across the sky. Blond hair rested on her bare shoulders which were defined like an Olympic swimmer. She grimaced. "Who is the, er, maid?"

Karlene smiled knowingly. "That's Candy. I'll explain all about her in a while. Once we've settled." She looked over at Candy. "Bring us coffee and be quick." She flicked her fingers and Candy curtsied and scuttled away. Gemma stared at Candy in continued bemusement.

Karlene showed Gemma across the open-plan floor to her corner sofa. Gemma sunk into the soft black leather. Karlene sat beside her.

A watery October sun flickered across the floor. It peered in through the floor-to-ceiling windows that ran around two sides of the room. Twenty stories below them, vehicles lined up along the wide streets, hustling and chugging forward. Triple-glazed windows blocked the autumnal chill of the wind blowing off the slow wide river in the distance.

"So," Karlene began and took Gemma's hands in hers. "Tell me about yourself, the woman who stole Paul's heart." She held on to the thought of him as Pansy. "Paul was my first." She didn't elaborate on first in what.

Gemma's face beamed, clearly assuming first boyfriend. Karlene warmed to her wholesome look. Naive but strong. A strange mix.

Gemma explained she had been a professional supermodel. She said at thirty-six, she found it difficult to find work, there were so many other young models coming up. She spent much of her time these days at the gym, keeping trim in case work came in. Otherwise, she socialised, usually at Paul's business events.

She said she guessed she had a nice time and she had the best loving man in the world as her husband. Maybe it wasn't a fulfilling life when Paul was not at home with her, she had so much more to offer. Paul earned so much money she didn't need to work. He provided for her, he cared for her.

Karlene listened to Gemma with interest, she liked her. Gemma told her they had met at a business event, fallen in love, and married within eight weeks. As she spoke about their marriage, Karlene saw how much they loved each other. What loving wife wouldn't want to make their secret sissy husband happy as a cuckold femboy in pretty little girl dresses once she knew his proclivity for being a sissy princess?

"Paul is always working to make a better life for us both. He wants the best for me, nothing is too much trouble for him if it makes me happy."

This was music to Karlene's ears. Once she had shown Gemma how to be the dominant goddess, Paul would be unable to refuse her anything. This made things easier. He'd be ecstatic to have a dominant wife who feminised and cuckolded him.

"He's so loving when at home." Gemma continued and looked up at Karlene, her eyes fresh, large and deep blue, her skin pure and unlined. "He brings me flowers, he takes me to dinner, he calls me throughout the day. He's so thoughtful. I couldn't have found a better husband."

"Yes, yes, I'm sure he's wonderful," Karlene said, her face turning serious. "But how are things? Sexually?"

Karlene spotted a flash of annoyance on Gemma's face. It passed in an instant and Gemma's face returned to her happy smile. Karlene guessed this was the weak spot, here was something to jemmy open wider.

At that moment, Candy arrived with a tray and coffee. She curtsied and scuttled away to the kitchen area.

Gemma's mouth opened and shut. Karlene smiled. "Remember, Gemma, I once dated Paul so I know he's not so big." She pointed to her crotch area. "Hence the question." She whispered conspiratorially, "Not so big down below." Karlene put two fingers up together with a small gap between them.

Gemma's face showed surprise. Then another hint of anger flashed on Gemma's face before her smile returned. "Everything is wonderful between us, Karlene. I have no complaints."

Gemma turned her face away which told Karlene she wasn't being honest. There was something in her face, her smile was watery, her eyes hid a touch of sadness.

Karlene persisted. "Yes I'm sure, darling, but I remember him being a little...., well, how should I put this? Girly. Did he tell you I used to call him Pansy?" She watched Gemma.

The annoyance flashed back in Gemma's face again then went back to her fixed smile. "No, he didn't," she said with a hint of annoyance. "Honestly, Karlene, it's great, he's great. I have zero complaints about anything to do with Paul. He must have changed since you knew him, it was a long time ago. He's perfect. Yes, he can be a little, I don't know. Less than masculine when he relaxes. But not everyone is super masculine. He's an important business leader."

Karlene nodded, she had opened the first crack in their so-called perfect marriage. The crack she would widen and lead to Gemma taking a lover. Gemma the Goddess and Pansy Princess her cuckold husband.

"So tell me, Karlene," Gemma said, still annoyed. "What is it you do?" She looked around and waved a hand in the air. "It looks like you're doing pretty well for yourself. This is some place. What is it? 8,000 a week rental?"

"I wouldn't know about the rental darling, I bought it outright."

"So what is it you do to afford a penthouse apartment in the centre of the city worth millions? Paul was vague about you and your work."

Karlene rubbed her chin and pursed her lips. "I'm a professional dominatrix.

The room went silent. Gemma's mouth dropped open for a moment. She snapped it shut.

"I emasculate men with big wallets and little dicks. I turn them into submissive sissy girls. They pay me because of their infatuation with being secret femboys. I let them live their fantasy for a few hours. Many are perfect housemaids and they pay me. Like Candy. She's a film producer by day although you wouldn't recognise her at the moment. This is how I afford a multimillion penthouse in the city."

Gemma's mouth dropped open again and remained open. Like a broken ventriloquist's doll. She looked towards the kitchen for Candy. "Candy is a man?"

Karlene leant in and took Gemma's hand in both of hers. "Not exactly, darling. Technically a male maybe, but a femboy. I have a passion, Gemma darling, a calling. I love to help wealthy males find themselves. What they're looking for is to become submissive sissies to alpha women. And they give me money for the privilege. Lots of money."

Gemma stared at Karlene with disbelief.

"I find real men for sex. I love those with small brains and big developed muscles on 6ft 4in plus bodies. Which is why I also like sensitive femboy sissies to serve me while I'm taking sexual advantage of real men. I get the sissies to clean up after and that kind of thing." Karlene looked at the ceiling with thoughts of passionate nights passing through her mind with sissies running around at her barked instructions "It's all very discrete, of course, and in private. Some of these sissies are well-known men in the media, politics, business and sports. You'd never imagine who wants my services." She hung on the last sentence. Would Gemma get her hint?

Gemma loomed back in astonishment.

"You can't imagine the pleasure I get from my work," said Karlene. "It's as if my body becomes filled with energy. It's like I'm super-charged. To see those once-powerful men creeping around as my submissive femboys." Karlene sighed in pleasure. It was time to plant the seed. "I'm sure once you've experienced a rock-hard eleven-inch cock filling your pussy or mouth." Karlene touched Gemma's lips with a fingertip, "there's no going back, darling. You'd love it. Especially when you have a sissy femboy, like Candy, to clear up after you."

Gemma was mute.

7 – It begins

"Let me explain, Gemma darling. I'm never cruel." Karlene continued. "This isn't about forcing but gentle persuasion and nudging. Many males want this. They want to be little girls, submissive sissies in pretty dresses. I have found most males have a sissy femboy inside them waiting for the right person to bring it out. That is where I come in."

A moment passed. Gemma's tight shocked face dissolved into a wide grin. "Karlene, you're such a joker. Paul told me you liked to joke and to shock and tease. Especially about sexual matters." Gemma chuckled but her eyes were not smiling.

Karlene could see Gemma didn't know if she was joking or not. "Remember darling, I dated Paul in college. He was my submissive pansy girl in private. We never had sex. We tried it a couple of times in the beginning but it was not satisfying for me. So I stopped it and took lovers. He knew and was sometimes there to watch and clear up after for me. He complained but he liked that really."

Gemma fidgeted, showing her discomfort. She pulled her hand away from Karlene's and stood up, her gaze shifted to the sky outside the picture windows. Karlene noted Gemma hadn't rejected her confession out of hand. She hadn't stormed out, she was thinking about what she'd heard. Something had intrigued her about Karlene's lifestyle.

Gemma turned back to face her. "This is all a shock to me. I live a traditional life with a wonderful man. I can't begin to comprehend this, this, this..." She walked to the window and swung back to face Karlene. Her blond hair flowed around her neck, flicking against her strong bare shoulders. The sun lit a glowing halo around her head. For a moment, Karlene's stomach turned cartwheels. Gemma was stunning.

"I don't know what to call this, Karlene. Perversion?" She folded her arms, her breasts bulging. "I have Paul, he's enough for me. I can't imagine doing these things to him. Making men dress like little girls?

Paul? Or me having another man, even if he were six-four with a massive cock. I only want Paul. There could never be anyone else for me."

Gemma stared out of the window and Karlene could see her thoughts had turned to her husband. Karlene needed to push a little harder. What fun this was and what a challenge Gemma was. All the sissy men she had ever met had been soft clay for her to mould. This time she had a real challenge. That's why she had come to this city.

"Let me tell you about my hot male studs," Karlene said. "I have a couple of 6ft. 4in. boyfriends – rippling hard muscles, testosterone overload, small brains and giant cocks. They do what they're told. Have you ever felt an eleven-inch cock?" Karlene waited but Gemma didn't respond. "Maybe you have but now it's just Pansy Paul's tiny little clitty rattling around inside you."

Gemma stomped to the sofa and picked up her handbag. "Enough, Karlene. How dare you insult my husband and insinuate our sex life is lacking. Paul is not a sissy. Everything is perfect, he is perfect, our marriage is perfect." She marched to the front door, her shoes clattered on the hardwood floor. She stopped at the front door as Candy rushed out to serve. Gemma threw her a look of distaste and she stopped and looked at Karlene for instructions.

Karlene raised a palm to tell her to wait.

"Karlene." Gemma composed herself. "There's something wrong with you." Gemma wiped a tear from her eye with the back of her hand.

Karlene guessed this would happen. She had gone in a little hard, but she wanted to stir Gemma into a reaction to soften her up.

"Let me out. I'm going home" Gemma stamped a foot on the wooden floor like an angry child. It echoed around the quiet apartment. Candy made to move to open the door but stopped dead on seeing Karlene's palm raised again.

Karlene got up and walked towards Gemma, her arms out. "Gemma, darling, I didn't mean to upset you. I'm so sorry. Please forgive me."

Karlene laid an arm across Gemma's strong shoulders. Skin touched skin. She kissed Gemma's cheek. Gemma looked confused, she hadn't expected that reaction.

"Gemma, darling, it's my work, I don't do anything bad. Everything I do is consensual and private. Do you think I forced Candy to come here and be my housemaid? No, she pays me to do this. Now. Come back and sit down with me. Please? Give me a chance to explain a little more. Hear me out."

Karlene took Gemma's hand and led her back to the sofa. Gemma's face was set in a look of petulance and she made a show of reluctance by dragging her feet. They sat back down and Karlene kept both her hands wrapped around Gemma's hand. She knew Gemma was intrigued. She shooed Candy away.

Gemma spoke. "I would never hurt my husband. Ever. I love him. The idea of having sex with someone else is abhorrent. Abhorrent, Karlene." She shook her head. "And to turn men into sissy femboys?" She shook her head again.

Karlene's thumb rubbed Gemma's hands. "I wouldn't expect anything different from you, darling. It's wonderful how much you love each other. But you wouldn't be hurting him. It's what he wants. He just needs you and me to help him. To give him a nudge into his promised land."

Gemma sobbed a little. Karlene guided Gemma's head onto her shoulder, rubbing her hair. Karlene rested a hand on Gemma's thigh, an inch above her knee. Gemma's stockings were soft and smooth. Karlene swayed her fingertips up and down Gemma's leg, down to her knee and back up to her dress hem. It soothed her and Gemma's sobs stopped.

Karlene rubbed her fingers up and back down to Gemma's knee. The next time she went higher, pushing the hem above patterned stocking tops. Gemma put her hand on Karlene's, stopping her from going further. She didn't push her away, she kept her hand over Karlene's.

Karlene put her lips to Gemma's ear, through soft shiny fair hair. She whispered. "It's so hot to turn a powerful man into a pansy princess, a cuckold sissy. And it's what they want. Everybody gets something from it."

Gemma relaxed and closed her eyes. Karlene pulled her hand out of Gemma's and moved it to her inner thigh. Her skin was delicate and uncovered by stockings. She moved a single fingertip in circling motions on the soft white skin above her stocking top. She moved, pushing the dress hem up with her fingers, hinting but not touching the two lip mounds outlined in the white panties. Gemma's dress was above her panties; her stocking suspender straps showed stark against Gemma's light skin.

"I tease and deny powerful men. I whisper to them they are little girls. Sissies. Can you imagine how erotic that is? And they are all married, Gemma darling. Their wives don't know what their husbands want so they get it from people like me."

Gemma nodded, her eyes closed. She arched her back. She got Karlene's insinuation this time. "My husband is paying for Mistresses?"

Karlene ignored her question. "The trick is to seduce them but never allow them to cum," said Karlene. "Denial is key, darling. When they are desperate to cum, I stop on the cusp and I tell them to talk like little girls. They do this thinking they will be permitted to cum. Sometimes I like them to develop a cute lisp – *yeth pleasth, Mistreth Karlene, I want to be a pwitty pwinceth,* they say. Of course, I never let them orgasm. Oh no. Not allowed ever."

Gemma sighed, her eyes remained closed tight. "I speak to them as if they were little girls because they are little girls. I tease and deny them until they are reduced to tears. I take their little foreskins on their little cockettes in my two fingers. I rub them up and down to the point of climax again. I sometimes scratch a fingernail up and down the back of their little clitties or rub their little hole at the end. It drives them crazy. They will do whatever I ask at this point. Would you like me to show you how I do that with Candy?"

Gemma shook her head vigorously. Karlene's brushed a finger against Gemma's vagina lips as she made circles on her inner thigh. Karlene's lips brushed Gemma's ear and she kissed it. Gemma groaned lightly.

"Imagine Pansy's little cockette is on the brink of bursting out sissy juice. Sissy arches her back and I take my fingers away. Again."

Gemma gasped. Karlene was pulling her in.

"I tell the sissies they have to beg like little girls to orgasm. They beg, they cry out. I watch as their cockettes relax and I then start again. Sometimes a little drop oozes out. I run a single finger under their clitties, from base to end, all the time telling them they are good little girls, pretty sissies. They're not men but helpless little sissy girls. I want them to admit they want to be sweet princesses. All the while I run my fingers along their tiny clitties, soft and slow. Then when they are about to burst again. I stop. I give them a moment to calm down and I start all over again. It's exquisite and they love being controlled and frustrated that way."

Gemma's legs opened and her mouth parted. Her breath became slow, as if she were asleep.

"They become so desperate, they sob gently like little girls, a mix of frustration and joy. I tell them to let it out. I say they are sweet sissy femboys and it's good to cry like the little girls they are. I smile at them and whisper in their ears. It's important to be gentle and caring with them. To a point. Then I'm not, but that's another story."

Karlene's circling finger brushed up against Gemma's vagina lips. Her legs were wide apart and her head lolled.

"At this stage, Gemma darling, my hand tightens on their girly balls. I twist and squeeze a little. Not too much but enough to make them squeal and know who's in charge. I rub a hand down their cheeks and wipe their tears away with a caring finger. I tell them they can cry, they are sissy princesses and they should let it all out. They need to cry. I smile at them, I rub their cheeks and they feel better. I turn them over and make them bend. I pull their panties down and slap them hard across their bottoms. With each slap, I whisper to say what a cute pansy they are, a sissy who will watch their wife with a real man. I tell them I will allow them going to swallow a real man's cum. They are sissy girls, so why not?"

Karlene pushed her finger against Gemma's light white panties, parting her damp vagina lips through the light cotton. Karlene felt her sticky warmth.

"Then I tell them they will have to learn to rub a real man's penis like the sissy sluts they are."

Through the panties, Karlene found the engorged bud at the top of Gemma's vagina. She brushed her fingertip against it, Gemma made a low whine, sucking in through her teeth.

"And you can do this with Paul too, darling. He's a sweet little pansy girl beneath his successful businessman veneer. I should know. He called me a couple of days ago asking me to make him a submissive femboy sissy not knowing it was me. He wants this, Gemma."

Gemma's eyes were closed. She shook her head and said in a soft voice. "No, Paul is my man, he's not a femboy...." She never finished her sentence. She pushed her hips forward into Karlene's finger and gave out a long slow, "*Oooooh,*" as she orgasmed.

Karlene's plan was going well. It was time to close in on the final stage.,the awakening of Gemma as a dominant Goddess and the transformation of Paul into the sissy princess he desired.

8 — The Affair

Gemma opened her eyes, looking sleepy and satisfied. She looked around as if not sure where she was. She blinked twice and came to. "Paul loves me and he cares for me, Karlene. I love him like crazy, I adore him."

Karlene continued to caress Gemma's vagina lips with a light touch. Gemma lay back, in a state of abandon.

"Yes, I know he loves you," Karlene said. "But Gemma darling, does he satisfy you with that tiny clitty?"

Gemma giggled, a low sexy sound. "Paul is a wonderful loving husband." She hesitated. "Not great in bed, I accept that. But it's not his fault he's tiny down there. It's a small price to pay for how he is in everything else."

Karlene's fingers moved away from Gemma's labia and she slid one finger inside her. "Do you like my finger, Gemma darling, it's bigger than Paul's little femboy dick. His little sissy clitty. You're getting more sensation from one of my fingers that his clitty."

Gemma smiled, her eyes distant. Karlene withdrew her finger and reinserted it again, slow and deliberate. She pushed in a little further inside, circling as she moved it in and out. Gemma was gushing wet.

"You could have something much bigger, much firmer inside you. A real cock, a real man's big hard erection. Eleven inches of hard rod."

Gemma put her hand on Karlene's arm. "No, I couldn't do that, not to my Paul."

Karlene put the end of her thumb onto Gemma's swollen bud while her forefinger remained inside her. "Have you ever heard of cuckolding, darling?"

Gemma shook her head but was no longer listening. Karlene loved the way Gemma groaned and twisted in enjoyment. She would return to the theme of large cock, tall muscled men and cuckolding in a while. Gemma would understand, it was a matter of time. She would introduce her to someone she knew soon. Someone tall, broad-shouldered with sculptured muscles and a long thick cock. Soon. Someone Karlene often used.

Karlene pressed her hand against Gemma's mount. Her finger danced inside Gemma's soaking vagina. Her thumb worked on her clitoris, circling and kneading against it, gentle and slow. Gemma's eyes rolled and she closed them again.

"Imagine, Gemma darling," Karlene whispered in her ear. "You, a strong beautiful goddess, turning your husband into the cuckold sissy femboy he wants to be. Teasing him, denying him until he accepts he's a pansy princess. You cuckold him with a big tall man with a body like carved marble and an enormous thick cock. Pansy Paul will weep, knowing how you're now satisfied sexually. He will cry tears of joy for you and tears of shame he can't satisfy you in that way. Your Pansy only wants what's best for you, he loves you. He will cry at his own failure, knowing he's just a silly little sissy femboy."

Gemma arched her back again, Karlene's fingers flitting and moving, damp and soft.

"How enchanting does that sound, Gemma darling? How hot, how exciting? Your husband Paul, a pansy princess wearing a little girl's party dress. It will be white, short and frilly. His panties will show beneath the hem and he will be in white ankle socks and have a pink bow in his hair. He will watch as your new boyfriend mounts you, pushing his giant cock deep inside you."

Gemma groaned softly.

"Then just as your stud is about to cum, you pull away. You slide down his body as Pansy watches. You pull your stud's swollen, engorged cock towards your lips, your smooth porcelain-white hands will gripped around it. Pansy Paul will see it all. You poke out your tongue to lap at the end of the huge straining erection. Pansy will sob knowing how happy and satisfied you are and how excited he is at being cuckolded. Believe me, he wants this. It's what I used to do for him."

Gemma's eyes opened a moment, hearing about her husband's previous life. They closed again as Karlene worked on her.

"You rub your slim long fingers down your new boyfriend's huge penis shaft, moving more quickly, your long nails dig into his full balls. Pansy's face will be horrified and fascinated as you close your lips around the end of the giant cock. Your stud will move his hips, sliding his cock in and out, fucking your mouth. It's now full of eleven inches of erect cock, down your throat. Imagine it when the stud jerks. You pull your lips away from your stud's raging erection and your mouth is open wide. You take your stud's straining erection and hold it to your open lips. Pansy sees your stud shoot jets of viscous white fluid into your open mouth. It falls onto your tongue and around your mouth, again and again until your stud has expended his load and slumps, exhausted, satiated."

Gemma writhed and groaned.

"You turn to your Pansy Princess who will be transfixed by what he saw. Loving and hating it at the same time. You slap his face and tell him he can never satisfy you like your new boyfriend."

Gemma squealed a short high sexual sound.

"You then tell him to clean up your stud's cum. You want this, Gemma darling, I know you do. Tell me you want it."

Gemma hummed a deep moan. Karlene's fingers twisted, twirled and flicked inside her. Karlene felt Gemma stiffen in climax. "Yes, yes, I want this." She said. "I can't do it to him, I shouldn't." She twisted in pleasure. "But I want it."

Karlene sat up. "Then I will teach you how we turn your husband into a cuckold sissy femboy."

Gemma's eyes sparkled.

"And Gemma darling," Karlene said. "Paul will thank you for this, it's what he desires desperately."

9 — Goddess

"Today, Gemma darling, I will teach you how to be a sexy goddess for your husband."

It was two days since Gemma had last been in Karlene's apartment. She had returned for the training. She was prepared to help her husband become a cuckold femboy. Karlene guessed Gemma still had some reservations about what she was proposing. She knew Gemma liked the concept of being a dominant sexy goddess, that was certain. She needed convincing that her husband was desperate for her to make him a sissy femboy. This was understandable and Karlene had to overcome that hurdle. It was a small hurdle.

It was morning and Gemma sat on the large sofa looking up at Karlene. Karlene asked how she felt about the intimate time they had spent last time. Did she feel she'd been unfaithful?

Gemma's face frowned a moment. "I think something so intimate between two strong attractive women was not being unfaithful. It happened and it was natural, not unfaithful."

This was a good sign. Karlene paced the floor in front of Gemma. She was graceful, measured and feline, a dark brooding panther on the prowl. She preferred to teach Gemma at her own home. It was her territory, her lair, and there would be no reminders for Gemma of her marriage to Paul. She needed to remove Gemma from her environment to let her see things more dispassionately.

Gemma had changed her clothing style under Karlene's instructions. Karlene had sent a long text of instructions explaining if Gemma was to become a sexy goddess, she needed to look the part. Today she was less the professional supermodel, more the stunning seductive sensual Goddess.

Karlene had two sissies in the apartment today for Gemma's training. They waited in a spare room.

Gemma wore a white mini-dress, it clung tight over her large breasts. The low-cut top displayed acres of Gemma's firm large breasts, a hidden bra pushing her cleavage up tight. Her breasts were like two giant melons pushed together. Her bare arms were defined and her shoulders sporty. Her time in the gym had been well-spent. She had pulled her blond shoulder-length hair lower over her forehead. It added a touch of mystery and allure.

Today, Gemma was more sexual and sensual. Their previous chat had worked.

Karlene had dressed in her dominatrix clothing. Not for her the black leather or latex. She was far too subtle to need the obvious. She believed you had to look the part, as well as act it. Karlene was more colourful than Gemma. Her skirt was a golden metallic-effect material and even shorter than Gemma's. The skirt had a bright thick waistband and six-inch-long strips of golden material hung from it. As she walked her legs protruded through, showing her long slim light-brown legs.

She wore a top which was more like a bra. It was the same metal effect as the skirt and looked like two golden hubcaps on her boobs. Matching strips of material hung from the bra. Her waist was long and slender. Her bare shoulders were covered by abundant luxuriant brown hair. A pair of large hanging earrings hung from her small earlobes and clinked together like wind chimes whenever she moved her head.

"Today, Gemma darling, I will also teach you how to make your strong, successful man into your submissive sissy. I will describe the methods and techniques I have learnt and refined over the past ten years. You will learn how to tease and deny him. This is an important control method. You will learn to use your sexy female wiles and your beautiful hands to force a man to behave like a demure sissy. I have Sissy Daisy and Sissy Lily today for you to practise on. Are you ready, darling?"

Gemma looked up at Karlene, a look of concern on her face. "Yes, but—"

Karlene paced the floor in front of the seated Gemma. "But what, darling?"

Gemma pursed her wide pronounced lips. "I love the idea, of course I do. But maybe Paul doesn't really want it. What if you're wrong? What if he's changed?"

Karlene stopped pacing and stood still. "OK, darling, I sense you're not yet convinced that Paul wants to be your obedient sissy. OK, for now, let's start your Mistress training and we'll come back to the Paul issue later. OK, darling?" She turned her head. "Daisy, Lily. Come here now."

Gemma's face brightened into a smile bordering on a laugh as two tall willowy sissies shuffled towards them. Daisy was tall and had what looked like a blond wig and wore a tiny pink pleated mini skirt. Lily was shorter and a little more solid. Her hair was brown and looked natural. She wore a pink layered ra-ra skirt no more than six inches long. Both wore thin tan stockings with smooth legs.

Karlene was going to have to work harder than she'd thought to get Gemma to turn Paul into the femboy she knew he was desperate to become. She knew Gemma would accept it in the end and getting her to work with Daisy was going to help her. In the meantime she would tread carefully, she didn't want to scare her off. One small step at a time.

Karlene opened her arms out. "Let's begin. By the end of the day, you will have all you need to become the super-sexy-vixen goddess I know you are. You will be equipped to fulfil your destiny in turning powerful men into sissy girls. "Karlene waited for an objection. None came, she wanted to plant her next idea into the training. "And as a sissy, he will crave to please and do anything you tell him. Including playing with other sissies."

Gemma moved her head, her eyebrows creased tightly together. She didn't comprehend.

Karlene started pacing again. "Yes dear, sissies love to play with each other's little poppets."

"Poppets?"

"Their little winkies, dear."

"But we're not talking about Paul, are we?"

"We'll see, darling, we'll see." The idea was planted. "I haven't met a sissy yet who doesn't want to be pretend forced to have sex with another sissy."

She indicated the two sissies approached her. She lifted their skirts and pulled down their little panties. Their penises went to erections instantly. Karlene took one in each hand and pulled the sissies together. She rubbed the ends of their erections together and both had a look of fake horror mixed with elation in their eyes.

"Kiss each other, girls," said Karlene as she rubbed the ends of their erections together.

They planted their lips together and kissed passionately. Gemma scrunched her eyes in disbelief and looked in wonder at Karlene.

Karlene clapped her hands and they stopped. "Daisy, on your knees and suck Lily's clitty until she cums in your mouth." She clapped once. "Now."

Daisy dropped to her knees and popped Lily's erection into her mouth and moved her lips up and down the penis.

Gemma stared with an open mouth as Karlene began to pace the floor again, explaining the techniques for becoming a sexy goddess while Daisy performed fellatio on Lily.

She explained how Gemma should wear sexy skimpy revealing clothes. This new style needed to be her daily wear from now on. It was a way to tease and deny, to make the femboys, like Daisy and Lily, more desperate. To see what they couldn't have.

"Your first task, Gemma dear, is to put away all your supermodel clothing. You will invest in a new wardrobe of sexier, more revealing clothes. Secondly, you will become even more sensuous in your movements and way of speaking. You're already sensuous, darling but now you're going to become even more so."

Lily groaned as Daisy jerked into her mouth.

Karlene explained that once Gemma was dressed erotically, she had to put the new sissy into little girls' clothes. It was important for Gemma to be sensual, luscious and voluptuous when transforming her sissy as she undressed him.

"They will want to grope you, to touch you as they will be desperate for you," Karlene explained. "Don't let them. Once you have undressed them, hold their balls and squeeze them. Not too hard but enough to show them you own them. Make the little pansy squeal like the little sissy he is. It's how males are, my darling Gemma. A switch goes on in their little heads when confronted by a sexy goddess, like you. Paul will be no different."

"But I thought we weren't talking about Paul?"

"I'm talking about all men, darling, and this includes Paul. That was all I meant." She looked at the two sissies. "OK, now I want you, Lily, to suck on Daisy's clitty. Don't let her cum as I want her for something else."

Lily said, "Yes Mistress," and Gemma nodded with a confused expression, her eyes were planted on the sissies as they swapped places. Gemma was still on her guard when it came to her husband but their floor show was distracting her.

"Pull on sissy's tiny dick and tell her how small it is. Tell her it's pretty and cute. You'd be surprised, but it will turn the little sissy on. Call the little penis a *clitty*. Because he is a girl now, he has a clitty not a cock. Just like Daisy and Lily here. Men have cocks, sissy femboys have clitties., don't you sissies."

"Yes Mistress Karlene," said Daisy dreamily while Lily grunted in the affirmative with Daisy's erection in her mouth.

Gemma nodded, taking it in with a stern look of concentration. That was good, thought Karlene, she was hooked.

"You'll tell sissy to put her arms up in the air. Let her stand there in front of you, naked with a little erection poking into the air. It will look so funny, you won't be able to resist giggling and pointing at the little clitty, all hard and desperate. Then you'll pull a little girl's short cotton dress over her raised arms and head. It will be in white or pink and with lots of frills. I find putting them in clothes suitable for six-year-old girls is the most suitable attire for my sissies, but anything extremely girly will work."

Lily pulled away from Daisy's erection. It stood out long and hard. "Lily, bend over, bottom in the air. Daisy, clitty in Lily's sissy vagina. Show Goddess Gemma what a good sissy femboy slut you are."

They both curtsied and said, "Yes Mistress," Lily bent over and Daisy sidled up behind her. She pushed her erection against Lily's anus and it slid in. Lily and Daisy gasped

Gemma nodded, her eyes unblinking at the scene in front of her. Daisy was slowly moving her erection in and out of Lily.

Karlene lost interest in her sissies. "Your sissy, Gemma darling, will feel the soft feminine material and want to cum as it flicks against her hard little clitty. She will be in a state of intense desperation. It's where you want her to be. Don't let him cum, ever. Unless it's with another sissy femboy. Like Daisy and Lily here. Tell her what a *pretty little girl* he is, Goddess's *pretty pansy princess*. The dress should never cover her little clitty; her dress must always be too short. Remember, they are femboys and not real girls or men."

Daisy was still sliding her erection in and out of Lily, her eyes rolling and she gave small moans. She was close to orgasm.

A wide grin came over Gemma's soft face. The corner of Karlene's lips curled in victory, she was getting through. Karlene's eyes sparkled. Gemma looked on in wonder at the two sissies performing sex for her and Karlene felt a spurt of electric exhilaration throughout her body. Pansy Paul's fate was settled. Gemma was transfixed

Soon she would have Gemma ready to turn Paul into the sissy femboy he was destined to become. No more skulking around with paid mistresses for a couple of hours of excitement. His beautiful sexy vixen of a wife would do this to him. Her first Mistress pupil was going to be a great success.

Daisy jerked and orgasmed. At the same time, Lily orgasmed and spurted her cum onto the wooden floor. They finished, hot and steamy. Daisy moved away, her flaccid penis hanging loose.

"Disgusting girls. You've made a mess on my floor. You'll both get down on your knees and lick up Lily's sissies juices this minute." She clapped her hands once and the two sissies jumped and then got down and started to lick the cum up.

Gemma looked at them utterly fascinated.

10 — Disdain

Karlene decided it was time for a break; time for Gemma to take in the lesson so far. Karlene told Lily to get up and get two glasses of sparkling water for them. Lily returned quickly with two ice blocks clinking in the bottoms of each glass and slices of cucumber floating around circular ripples on the tops. She curtsied as Karlene and Gemma sat, The two ladies sipped on the ice-cool water in silence.

The rain clouds outside the large windows were clearing. The sun glinted through the triple-glazed glass windows casting sharp beams across the room. Motes danced in the shafts of sunlight.

They drained their glasses together, throwing back their rich luscious hair in unison. They placed the empty glasses down on the walnut coffee table. It was time to continue with the lesson, refreshed and ready to restart.

Karlene shooed the two sissies away. "Disappear." She turned back to Gemma. "So, Gemma darling, you've put your sissy in a little girl's dress. She will look pretty and cute. You should continue to play with her little clitty and girly balls. Put your sexy hands under his skirt and fiddle, tease and play about with the little clitty. They love this and it makes them desperate. Once you've got them desperate for several months, it will be easy to make them do what Daisy and Lily have just done for your amusement."

Gemma giggled.

"You'll use a soft sweet tone and tell sissy *she* is a good little girl. *She* is your sissy princess. You must always reinforce the fact she has become a femboy princess. I stress, you need to do this through repetition and demonstration. Call her pansy, princess, petal, flower and any sweet girly name that comes to mind."

Gemma swallowed, her mouth was dry again.

"Be a little rough and be gentle with his clitty," Karlene said. "Stroke it lovingly, let it get excited, then pull hard and twist one way and the other. All the time you should be smiling, talking, telling *her* how pretty *she* is, how *she* is your adorable little girl, She's your cute cuckold princess. You'll stroke her erect clitty and tell her how cute it is. *She* will squeal and be in awe of you. She will be desperate for you, *she* will be like soft clay in your sexy hands.

She will put out *her* arms, your little girl will reach out, trying to caress you, trying to touch you. You need to bat *her* away with a loving disdain. You don't need to be cruel about it. You're a loving caring Goddess and you're doing all this for *her*. Because *she* is a pansy princess, she is not a real man. And she wants this badly. Why else would she be paying for it from a stranger?

You'll be loving, gentle and caring, but you also need to be firm and strict with her too. After all, *she* is your submissive femboy sissy. Remember, Gemma darling, you're doing a man with a small dick a massive favour. Powerful men with little dicks are so much better when they become little girls. Paul is not a man, not really. And he doesn't want to be. In his mind, he's a femboy and a sissy. He no longer admits it, but he did before he met you. Ten years ago, he admitted it to me as he wept and failed to satisfy me sexually. He told me he was a femboy and wished he could stay that way always. He will admit it again, Gemma darling. It's what he wants. Paul wants to be Pansy Princess again.."

Gemma went to speak and Karlene held up a hand of apology. "I know you didn't want to bring Paul into this, but he was such a good sissy boy back in college. It's how he is and should be again. You need to hear this and understand it, Gemma darling. Paul wants to be a *sissy princess* again. It's his destiny. It's for him to show his love for you and your love for him. Make him a sissy girl again, Gemma. For him."

Before Gemma could reply, Karlene continued to explain her techniques. She had planted the seed again of Paul being a sissy.

"So now you have Paul in pretty little girls' dresses with pretty ankle socks. You will force him to talk and giggle like a little girl."

"Paul?" Gemma interrupted. "I thought you were talking about powerful men in general? Paul's not part of this."

"I'm making it more personal, darling. Building pictures in your mind."

"In what way?" Gemma's voice showed a touch of irritation.

"Don't worry, darling, just absorb what I'm teaching you." Karlene continued. "You will make him speak like a little girl by using your fine sexy hands and fingers to play with his sissy clitty and pansy balls. Tease until he speaks like a little girl. Let me call out Lily and show you." She turned and shouted, "Lily. Here."

"But who's him, Karlene? Who exactly are we talking about here? Paul?"

Karlene made a brushing movement with an elegant hand. "You want to get him to tell you he wants to be a sissy boy who plays with other sissies." Lily scuttled towards them and curtsied and waited for instructions.

Gemma looked confused. "Why do we want him to play with other sissies, Karlene?"

Karlene sat down next to Gemma and took her hand. "Because it's what all powerful and important men with a femboy fantasy want." She thought for a moment. "It's what we want from them too. It's the best of both worlds." She looked at Lily. "It's what you want, don't you sissy slut? To have sex with other sissy boys."

Lily curtsied. "Yes, Mistress."

Gemma nodded. Karlene lifted Lily's dress and pulled down his panties to his knees. She grabbed and held his penis. "Watch this, Gemma." She started to rub Lily's penis and it grew. "So, sissy Lily," she said. You're a sissy femboy and no good to me. Unlike my big hot boyfriends. You can't be like them because you're an effeminate sissy slut and not a man." She looked up at Gemma. "Paul will love seeing you enjoy yourself with a real man, just as Lily likes to see me enjoy myself with a real man."

Karlene waited a moment to see if Gemma noticed she had used Paul's name again. Gemma said nothing. She continued.

"Sissy sluts like you, Lily, play with other sissy's clitties while real men make love with me. Gemma, your Pansy will also learn to love the taste of sissy juice and he will love to swallow every drop. You see, my dear. Paul is a sissy boy. But I think you know already."

"You're talking about my Paul, Karlene. I told you not to. I won't do that to him and he would never agree to it." Gemma shuddered. "My Paul? Playing with other men? No. He's not like that. He only wants me, not some sissy of yours with a small dick. He's not a pansy, he's an important businessman."

Karlene dropped Lily's erection. She took Gemma's smooth hand in both of hers. She rubbed her long white fingers with her own smooth dark fingers.

"Your hands are perfect tools for the task ahead of you. You can control any so-called powerful man and turn him into a little girl. I imagine Paul is already entranced by your hands, am I right Gemma?"

Gemma looked down with a sheepish grin. "Yes." Her voice was low.

Karlene took her hand and wrapped it around Lily's erection. "Imagine this is your husband. Pansy Paul."

Gemma snapped her hands away, her face hard, her forehead creased. Something in her eyes told Karlene that Gemma was exaggerating her anger. Was she finally getting through to her? She thought so.

It was time for the close.

11 — The Trainee

It was time for Karlene to push home the advantage she had carved out.

"Imagine, Gemma darling, how sexy it would be to use your sexy hands to take your sissy's trembling hands and force them to touch other sissies. To push her hands around a little erect clitty-like penis and rub it slowly up and down like a good princess. You'd be his guide."

Karlene squeezed Gemma's hand. She didn't pull it away, her eyes were wide and her lips parted. "Let's practise." She smiled. "Sissies. Out here now."

Lily and Daisy scooted to stand in front of the two ladies and curtsied in sync.

Karlene ignored them. "And all the while, Gemma darling, you tell Pansy Paul how you want her to be friendly with another pretty sissy. You tell her how you know she wants a sissy clitty in her mouth and in her sissy vagina. It's what sissies want, you saw that with these two." She threw a hand vaguely in the direction of Daisy and Lily. "It's what Pansy Paul wants. It's what he pays other Mistresses to do to him. It's time for you to take control of that. To give Pansy Paul what she wants and to find what you want too."

Gemma was listening enraptured, looking into Karlene's eyes. Gemma's free hand closed around Karlene's and they locked together in a mutual goal. Gemma never contradicted Karlene's use of female pronouns *her* and *she* for Paul.

Karlene turned to the two sissies. "Sissies kiss and hug each other like the sweet little girls you are. I want to see you sucking each other's tongues and grasping each other's bottom cheeks."

Daisy moved in to kiss Lily on the lips. Their tongues shot out and they licked them. Daisy sucked on Lily's tongue then locked open lips and they kissed passionately with their hands groping each other's bottom cheeks.

Karlene watched contentedly for a few moments. "This is how I expect my femboy sissies to behave. It's how you will now make Paul. We'll show her how to swoon at the sight of a pretty clitty."

Karlene clasped Gemma's hands tighter as the sissies kissed each other passionately. Sucks and squeals coming from them from time to time.

"You'll guide Pansy Paul's head close to a pretty sissy's lips, to lock lips with her. And you and your hunky boyfriend will watch them."

Gemma sat back. "What hunky boyfriend?"

Karlene kept hold of her hands. "You need a real man, Gemma darling. A man who can take care of your sexual needs in the way Pansy Paul never has and never could. And it's for Paul too. He wants to be cuckolded by you, he knows he can't give you what you want. Remember, it's what I did to him at university and he was happy for me."

"Really, Karlene?" Gemma was wide-eyed.

"Yes of course. And now it's your turn to assist Daisy and Lily." She stood and pulled the kissing sissies apart. And manoeuvred them to stand facing each other. They looked at each other in trepidation that Karlene knew was an act.

She pulled their panties to their knees and two erections stood out to attention. Karlene took Gemma's hand and led her to stand by the sissies. She put Gemma's hand around Daisy's erection and the other around Lily's. Lily let out a sigh of desire. With her hand over Gemma's, she pulled the two sissies' clitties together to rub against each other. She let go of Gemma's hand to leave her to do it. Gemma sniggered as she slid the end of each rock-hard sissy clitty against each other.

"You'll rub Pansy Paul's sissy cockette with the little cockette of another sissy just like you're doing now. You and your boyfriend will watch and laugh and call Pansy Paul a slutty sissy."

Karlene stood by Gemma smiling as the two sissies groaned in pleasure. "Use your sexy hands to make Daisy get down on her knees."

Gemma leaned on Daisy's shoulder and she knelt in front of Lily's erection.

"Now use your beautiful elegant hand to push Daisy's mouth onto Lily's clitty."

Gemma took Daisy's head. She opened her mouth wide and Gemma guided her onto Lily's waiting erection. Daisy moaned a gurgle.

"And with your other hand…."

Karlene raised Gemma's other hand.

"You will hold and rub your stud's cock. You will make Pansy swallow the other sissy's juice, licking the end clean making sure there are no drips. Like a lollipop."

Karlene licked her lips as Gemma pushed and pulled Daisy's blond head up and down by her hair.

"You, my sexy friend, Goddess Gemma, will use words of encouragement, telling Pansy, "*Good sissy femboy,*" as she swallows the sissy juice. Tell her, "*A good sissy femboy slut must always swallow her sissy girlfriend's juices,*" as she licks up the last drop of cum. Do that when Daisy cums and imagine it's Pansy"

At that moment, Daisy came into Lily's mouth. As she jerked cum into Lily's mouth, Gemma said, "Good sissy femboy, swallow all your sissy girlfriend's sissy juice. Good sissy."

Daisy finished and pulled her limp clitty from Lily's mouth. Cum hung from her lips and on her cheeks.

"Lick it all off, sissy slut," Karlene said to Daisy. She leant down and licked and sucked her cum from Lily's face and lips.

"You will tell Pansy how grateful *she* should be. You will tell *her, she* had been hiding in her femboy closet for far too long." Karlene pointed at Gemma. "And you, Pansy's hot sexy wife, have dragged her out into the open. Pansy will be overcome by gratitude. No more paying professionals for a business transaction. Pansy will have a loving sexy wife to help turn her into a femboy sissy slut."

Gemma sat wide-eyed in fascination.

"Once Pansy has finished, you will make her say, "*Thank you, sir,*" to your hot stud for satisfying you, Pansy's wife. You will make Pansy tell you and your hot boyfriend how much *she* loves being your sweet femboy princess and serving you both."

Gemma looked back at Karlene in wonder. A fleeting smirk passed Karlene's lips, she knew she finally had Gemma's full buy-in.

"You will be a sexy dominant goddess, Gemma dear. You will transform Pansy Paul into the sissy princess he is desperate for." Karlene tightened her grip around Gemma's hand. "Pansy will become a much better person. A sissy femboy. She will become your princess to tease and play with in ways you can only imagine now. You'll be doing all this for your love for Pansy. *She* will complain at first, but don't let it put you off. It's what *she* wants even if *she* doesn't realise it at first. *She* will understand in time and become like Daisy and Lily. She will thank you for what you have done to *her*. And don't worry, Gemma darling, I will be there to guide you."

Gemma stared at Karlene with her mouth in a wide circle of wonder. Now to consolidate the process and teach Gemma her next stage: how to make her husband into the perfect cuckold princess. Cuckold her with a stud of a man and with me.

Karlene moved up close to Gemma's dreamy face. She could smell her rich sweet perfume, the faint tang of minty toothpaste. She gazed at the tiny laughter lines around the outside corners of Gemma's large blue eyes. They were the only lines on a face that seemed to be made of porcelain. She kissed her lips lightly and they stayed locked together for several moments.

They broke the kiss and Karlene stared into Gemma's eyes. "So, Gemma darling, are you ready? Ready to turn your husband into a submissive and cuckold femboy princess?"

12 — Breakthrough

Gemma sat up. She had been relaxing, listening to Karlene, taking in her words and chewing them around in her mind. "Karlene, I'm curious. What you've told me appeals. A lot. And what you have told me about Paul, rings true."

Karlene felt a surge of excitement inside her. She fought the desire to wave her arms in the air, to shout, "*Woo-hoo*," in celebration. She knew but people sometimes won't accept what's in front of their eyes. She held her joy in. "Gemma darling, It's time to stop calling her Paul and use Pansy. It's what I called her in college, both in private and in public. It's more appropriate for what she is beneath that thin masculine veneer."

Gemma's face was set seriously and hard. Karlene saw something had changed inside her. Gemma didn't dispute her renaming suggestion. She guessed Gemma was about to unload some of her secrets. She had gained Gemma's trust.

"You are right, Karlene," Gemma blurted out as if her dam had burst. Paul can be girly."

Karlene's eyebrows raised. "Paul? Or did you mean Pansy, darling?"

The two women laughed together, a shared joke, a shared experience.

"Don't get me wrong," Gemma said. "He's the most wonderful man in the world. A loving and caring husband, but..."

Karlene stared at Gemma, unblinking, nodding gently. She didn't want to interrupt her now she was unloading. She rubbed a hand down Gemma's bare arm. She held her hand and bent down to kiss her fingers.

Gemma looked down, her cheeks flushed red. "He sometimes cries like a little girl when we have sex. Or when he has sex. I feel very little physically." She wiped an eye with one long delicate finger. Was there a tear? Gemma looked up, her face dry, it had been a fleeting image.

Gemma sat up tall. She looked stronger, as if something had changed inside her. She was more confident and assertive. In control of her emotions.

"Paul, Pansy." Gemma giggled nervously at saying her husband's sissy name. "Pansy is submissive in bed, I have to take charge. I have to be on top, he's passive. He cums in seconds. It's unsatisfying. You were right, Karlene, sex with Pansy is unsatisfying." She looked up. "I love him, her, deeply. Now I know what I need to do for me and for him. I can become the dominant Goddess for him, you spoke about. It's how I am and I have always felt it. I held it in before."

Karlene rubbed Gemma's arm again. "Yes, you are an alluring Goddess, darling, I saw it from the moment we met. You will drag Pansy Paul out of his sissy closet. We will do it together, I'll be there for you, Gemma darling, to help, guide and support you. You won't need to do this alone, you have my full support and love."

They were united in their shared objective, their sexy hands entwined. They kissed again.

"You need to think of Paul as a sissy femboy. Her name is Pansy. Use only female pronouns - *her, she*. From now on, no more references to Pansy Paul as a male, ever. She is now a *sissy*, a femboy, a *pansy princess*. OK? Pansy will be surprised at first and may even seem to fight it but that's her societal programming kicking in. She'll soon grow to adore the new life because it's the life she craves."

"OK, Karlene."

Karlene saw a new light burning in Gemma's eyes. She had experienced an epiphany. "And darling, you must remember, Pansy Princess will struggle and fight back. She won't want you to transform her into a sissy at first. You're going to have to guide her to her destiny with a loving, but firm direction. Are you ready to do this? To push her to what is best for her?"

Gemma nodded, her hair flailing over her face in her enthusiasm.

"Good. Resistance is normal, they all do it or pretend to do it. Pansy Paul will pretend too. You will have to work through this phase. It will be difficult at times and you'll doubt yourself. You need to be strong. You'll have second thoughts when Pansy stomps her feet and complains she doesn't want to be a sissy."

Gemma nodded.

"This will spice up your sex life, Gemma darling, and give you both a new thrill and an exciting life together. You as the Goddess and your husband as the submissive femboy sissy. I know you're going to be the hottest heartbreaking cuckolding wife in the world. Believe me, darling."

"Thank you, Karlene, you're such a good friend."

The two women held hands in mutual respect and Gemma ran a hand in Karlene's hair. Their lips touched and their tongues flicked together. Two dominant ladies, two stunning goddesses.

Gemma looked up at Karlene and kissed her cheek. "I understand what I need to do, I don't know where to start?"

"That's normal, darling. It's a set of stages. I won't be with you all the time, I'm your mentor."

Karlene got up and walked to a writing desk in the far corner of the large room. She picked up a notepad and a pencil and returned. Gemma watched her, the eager student. Karlene passed her the book and pencil. She told her to make a list of what she needed to do to prepare for her husband's transformation into a sissy princess. She waved the two waiting sissies away and they disappeared to the far room and shut the door.

"The first thing you need to do is to remove Pansy from the marital bedroom and give that sissy of a husband her a pink princess bedroom," Karlene said.

Gemma looked up then back down and wrote:

1. Give Pansy her own pretty bedroom.

"You will choose a small bedroom in your home and get a decorator in to paint it girly pink. You'll buy a single bed with a white frame and a soft pink headboard. You will buy bed clothes designed for little girls. The sheets will be pink, the pillow covers pink with large floppy frills. The bed covers will be in pinks and whites and other pastel colours. You should choose covers with images of cats, cartoon princesses and pretty little girls. They should be the type of covers pansy princesses love."

Gemma nodded and added to her list, her tongue protruding from her lips in concentration:

2. Paint bedroom walls light pink.

3. Get a single bed, with a soft pink headboard and white frame.

4. Pink frilly bed clothes suitable for little girls.

5. A bed-cover with pictures of cats, cartoon princesses and cute little girls

Karlene was pleased to see Gemma concentrating and taking her teaching seriously by taking notes.

"I suggest you buy soft cuddly toys and dolls to scatter over the bed. Sissies like that kind of thing. Some pretty cushions too, with little cats or cute dogs on them."

Gemma scribbled in her notebook, head down, concentrating.

6. Soft toys for Pansy.

Karlene continued. "You'll need a little girl's wardrobe unit for her new pretty girl's clothes. It needs to be a small double with a full-length mirror on the door so she can see how pretty she looks dressed up as a sissy princess."

Gemma wrote furiously.

7. Little girl's wardrobe

"Once you have had her bedroom decorated and furnished, you will fill it with girls' magazines. Pansy has to think as a girl and she needs to be reminded regularly. You will put up posters around the walls of cartoon princesses, cute animals and good-looking young men with bare muscled chests. Some of the men should be naked displaying their sexy penises.

Never forget, darling, as a cuckold sissy, Pansy's days of having sex with you or any other woman are over. She will only be allowed to ejaculate with other sissies. So, you will need to fill Pansy's life with constant reminders she is a sissy girl."

Karlene waited while Gemma finished adding to her to-do list.

8. Girl's magazines

9. Photos and posters of cute animals and young men.

"We need to talk about getting you a hot sexy boyfriend. A real man for a goddess like you."

Gemma stopped writing and looked up from her notepad. Karlene spotted a flicker of doubt flash through Gemma's eyes. This next step was possibly the biggest of all. She was now going to ask Gemma to cuckold the man she loved. It was an important step so she had to push on and overcome Gemma's doubt. She had Gemma's attention, she couldn't lose her now.

"You have to show your pansy husband that not only is *she* a sissy princess, but also *she* is not man enough for you. This is one reason you have to take a real man. The other is for your sexual satisfaction."

Karlene paused. The apartment was in silence.

"*She* is not man enough sexually. *She* needs to see and hear you being sexually aroused, pleasured and satisfied by a real man. It's the only way *she* will understand and accept her place in life as your pansy princess."

Gemma scratched an ear with the flat end of her pencil. She was thinking about this information and considering the implications. Karlene felt she could hear the cogs of Gemma's mind turning over. She knew a flicker of conflict remained in Gemma's mind over taking a lover and cuckolding her husband.

Karlene pushed on, she couldn't give Gemma time to dwell on this. She was so close to closing her plan.

"Gemma, dear, I know the perfect boyfriend for you. Someone looking for a new girlfriend. He'll be perfect for you."

Gemma perked up. "Who, what's he like? Tell me more." Anticipation burned in her wide blue eyes.

"In time, Gemma darling, in time."

Karlene didn't yet want to disclose that although the man she had in mind for Gemma was a yoga instructor and a porn star although she may keep that a secret for now. Once Gemma saw him, it wouldn't matter because he was big, well-hung with incredible endurance. Gemma looked disappointed, wanting to know more about this mysterious new boyfriend Karlene had found for her.

"You will love him, darling, I can guarantee it. Anyway, you will love having a sexy hunky boyfriend so much, you will want to move him into your master bedroom. That way, Pansy will better see and comprehend her inadequacy as a man. She will understand she is just a submissive sissy princess. She will see through the physical comparison with your hot stud what she is: an inadequate girly boy in a short pretty dress.

Gemma put the pencil between her lips. Her lips circled around the pencil. Karlene had an image of Gemma's luscious sensual lips around her husband's little dick. The pencil was about the same girth. It was much longer though. It was no surprise Gemma had jumped at her plan for feminising her husband so readily.

"Gemma dear, if you have any doubts, imagine this pencil is Pansy's clitty; insignificant. You feel nothing when it's inside you. Then imagine your lips are around an erect eleven-inch cock; hard, firm and filling your mouth. Imagine protruding into your cheek, tickling your tonsils. Imagine your tongue around the thick masculine head of firm cock."

Karlene sat next to Gemma and caressed her cheek. "Sounds good, doesn't it."

Gemma thought for a second. Her face hardened in determination. "Yes it does, Karlene." She took the pencil out of her mouth.

"I know the perfect man for you, Gemma darling. I know you'll love him and of course, he'll adore you. You're sexy and beautiful, far too much of a sexy Goddess for a silly sissy husband to satisfy. You need this real man. And he needs you."

Gemma thought for a moment. "Thank you, Karlene, for showing me the real Paul. I suppose I did know what he was like, if I'm honest. He is a femboy."

Karlene creased her eyes and forehead. "He?"

Gemma giggled. "Oh yes, I mean *her*." She smiled an alluring sexy smile, a new sexual desire was spreading over her. "I submerged the fact she had a tiny penis and she cried whenever we had sex. I tried to push to the back of my mind that she came too quickly and didn't satisfy me. You have shown me she is a submissive sissy. She will become my pansy princess and serve me and my boyfriend. Pansy buried this femininity inside her and we must bring it out."

Karlene added, "And remember, darling, this is for both of you. You are now the alluring Goddess Gemma. Soon, Princess Pansy will become the little sissy she closed up inside for too long. She will, once again, become Pansy I knew from college."

Gemma sat determined and placed her hands on her knees. "So we're ready then? When do we start?"

"Not quite, Gemma dear. There is a final stage we have touched on but haven't yet discussed in detail. Let's take a break and continue after lunch. We'll go out. I know a nice little French restaurant over the road. We'll continue the final lesson this afternoon."

Karlene got up and went to the front door and grabbed her coat. Gemma joined her and put on her coat. Karlene opened the front door of her apartment and looked back at Gemma.

"The final stage of this lesson, my beautiful sensual friend, is the final element. It will complete your Pansy's flowering into a sissy princess and you into the sexy alluring Goddess."

Gemma held her hands together and rubbed them as if washing them. "Oh do tell me now."

"After lunch, darling." Karlene smiled and walked through the door. Gemma followed. Karlene clicked the door shut behind them. She couldn't disguise the smile on her face.

13 — The Final Stage

The two women returned from lunch. Karlene disappeared to speak to the two sissies and Gemma scanned through the books in Karlene's oak bookcase. Gemma pulled out a paperback, *How I Feminised My Husband* by Lady Alexa. She skimmed through it and placed it back. She took out another, *Feminized and Pretty 1*, also by Lady Alexa.

"My favourite author," Karlene said as she walked back to Gemma. "I get many of my ideas from her books. I also find them rather hot, if I may be so open."

Gemma was reading some passages.

"Please take a couple, Gemma darling. I think you'd enjoy them."

Gemma thanked Karlene and held on to *Feminized and Pretty*. "This one looks like fun."

Gemma had changed, a sense of power and assurance rising over her. Karlene watched her with satisfaction at a job well done so far. Karlene had not discussed her teaching over lunch, she preferred to relax and get to know her new friend better. And to keep her powder dry for the final lesson; the cuckolding of Paul Paige.

The final stage was a crucial one for her plan. The complete transformation of Paul Paige from successful powerful business leader and secret sissy to an out-in-the-open cuckold sissy. A sissy who sucks on other sissy clitties and watches while his wife has sex with real men.

Karlene braced in anticipation, wrapping herself with her long slim arms. Her fingers held her arms, long red nails against light brown blemish-free skin.

Karlene let the silence grow. There had been a downpour during their lunch as men in the restaurant turned their heads and swivelled their eyes towards them throughout their lunch. The waiter had hovered too long, asking if everything was OK, if they were enjoying lunch. He had been too attentive, his eyes on stalks at the sensuous couple. They were two stunning attractive young ladies in skimpy sexy clothes in a heated humid restaurant. Outside, beyond the steamed-up windows, the rain had fallen.

Karlene looked across the room and watched the grey clouds racing across the sky. Gemma broke the silence.

"The final stage, Karlene? Tell me?"

Karlene put both her arms out full length and held Gemma's upper arms. She stared into her eyes.

"You'll need to follow my teaching to the letter, darling. This final stage is the roof over the entire process we've spoken about. Without it, everything else is an empty shell. This final stage is fundamental."

Gemma waited with anticipation.

"Karlene said. "Let's sit. I'm going to teach you how to make your husband into a full-time femboy. It's not just words, neither is it a game. Pansy will be walking the walk, as the rather crude but appropriate phrase goes."

Karlene guided Gemma back to the sofa. Gemma sat while Karlene remained standing. She felt energised talking about turning powerful men into gay sissies. "Gemma, darling, we've spoken about how you need to have a real man as a boyfriend. How you need to be sexually satiated in the way a goddess like you should be. And we've spoken about how Pansy will learn to have sex with other sissies."

Gemma didn't object. Karlene knew she had persuaded Gemma of her plan. She pressed on.

"This final stage, darling, comes after we have turned Pansy into a gay sissy princess. We've spoken about how she will play with other sissies like a good girl and we've practised with Daisy and Lily."

Gemma nodded agreement, her face open and ready.

Karlene's eyes narrowed. "What do you think is still missing, Gemma dearie?"

"I don't know, Karlene. It all seems pretty good. What on Earth more could we do to him, sorry I mean *her*."

Karlene breathed in. "For this final stage, you need to cuckold Pansy."

Karlene let this news sink in.

"You have to cuckold Pansy. She has to see and hear you having passionate loving sex with your new hunky boyfriend. This will be the concluding act of Pansy's transformation into a sissy princess and your transformation into the alluring Goddess."

Karlene frowned, furrowing her forehead to show Gemma this was an important point.

"This is what you'll learn this afternoon. How to cuckold your pansy princess. Are you ready?"

"I'm ready," said Gemma.

What she didn't know was that Karlene had a surprise for her. A massive surprise.

14 — The Big Lesson

"Once you have your new hunk of a boyfriend, you will introduce Pansy to him. Before your boyfriend arrives, we will then dress Pansy in the most girly type of clothing possible. We'll spray lots of perfume over her and make her face up with lipstick and eyeshadow. We will put her in the cutest little pink dress. Chiffon is nice, it's so fine and feminine. Her dress will be so short it won't cover her panties. It will be full of frilly sissy pleats and folds. I will provide something for her with writing on the front of the chest. It will say *Mummy's little princess,* or something similar. She will look so cute. I have plenty of little girls' clothing, I will give you a suitcase to take home with you tonight."

Gemma listened with her mouth open in wonder.

"Pansy will have cute white shoes, flat or low heels because she's a little girl. Only real women have sexy heels. They will have straps that buckle up. We'll put a huge pink bow in her hair. What do you think, darling?"

Gemma put her hands between her knees, her short skirt was high up her thighs and her cheeks were flushed with sexual desire. The idea of cuckolding her soon-to-be pansy princess was proving a huge turn-on for Gemma.

"OK, time to practise, Gemma darling."

"Practise?" asked Gemma.

Karlene nodded with a devious smile. At that very moment, the door buzzer sounded from someone at the entrance downstairs. Gemma looked concerned.

"A guest, darling." Lily scampered to the door and buzzed the guest in.

Gemma shifted on her seat. She wasn't keen on this sudden intrusion. Karlene continued to smile deviously.

The sound of the lift coming up sounded faintly from behind the door. It stopped. Heavy footsteps sounded to the door and there was a loud rap. Gemma jumped. Lily opened the door and curtsied, head down.

A huge muscled man walked in, the top of his head barely an inch below the door frame. His tight black hair was cropped short. His large black face looked as if it had been chiselled from marble. He wore a black round-neck tee shirt that look like it might burst at the chest. His arms were huge and so muscled he was unable to hang them down and they hung out like a gunslinger.

"We will make Pansy curtsey to Frank like Lily did. When she curtsies well, you'll tell her she's a good sissy princess and stroke her face and her little clitty." Karlene ushered Frank to her while Lily closed the front door. He towered over the two women like a giant skyscraper.

"You have to programme Pansy to understand reward and punishment. Bad behaviour gets a spank. Good behaviour gets a gentle stroke on her tiny clitty." Karlene grabbed Lily and lifted her dress. She had no panties on. Karlene stroked Lily's penis with one finger. "Good sissy, that was a perfect curtsey to Mr Frank. Now ask him if he'd like a drink, good girly."

Lily looked up into the huge brown eyes of Frank. "Would you like a drink, Mr Frank?" She curtsied.

Karlene stroked Lily's penis with a finger again and whispered in her ear. "Good sissy." She turned to Gemma. "Good behaviour gets a little sissy clitty stroke. Rewards."

Frank shook his head.

"This is what we'll be looking for from Pansy."

Gemma laughed, throwing back her head. Karlene liked to see her so relaxed.

"But that's not all, darling. You will keep telling her she's such a sweet pansy, a cute princess with a tiny clitty nothing like Frank who's a real man. Pansy will blush. This is good, she has to blush when she curtsies to your boyfriend, she's a femboy with an insignificant sissy clitty and Frank's a big strong masculine man."

Karlene spotted Gemma's eyes on Frank's crotch. There was a huge bulge in his trouser front.

"If you tell Pansy off, you tell her she's a naughty sissy. She must blush and say sorry Goddess Gemma. Spank her bare legs, then rub them to relieve the stinging while she cries. When she is good and you praise her. You tell her she's a good pansy princess and stroke her little clitty. Make her blush and giggle. Make her curtsey over and over and over until she gets it right, all the time blushing and giggling. And don't forget the reward when she does it well. You stroke her face and tickle and fondle her little clitty as a reward. Not to cum but as a reward, nothing more. If she fails, slap her face, her legs and her clitty and pussy balls."

Gemma beamed with a broad smile. "I'm looking forward to this, Karlene, it all sounds excellent."

"We now have your Pansy husband in pretty princess clothes. She can curtsey like a good sissy and she blushes and giggles. We force her to stand in front of your new boyfriend and curtsey. She will address Frank as Sir."

"Sir?" Gemma said.

"Pansy must call him Sir, and you are Goddess Gemma. She is to call me Mistress Karlene"

"That's a bit odd, isn't it? Goddess? I'm his wife."

No, Goddess is a perfect title, she will be your sissy, what else should she call you?"

Gemma pondered this and agreed.

"So, your hunky boyfriend Frank arrives as he has just done. arrives, Pansy will curtsey and she must giggle and blush. She must swivel from side to side holding out her pretty dress."

Karlene raised her eyebrows to Lily who swivelled side to side as she'd described. She saw Gemma's eyes had not strayed from Frank's crotch. She looked up at Frank. "Frank, be a good boy and undo your flies and get out your dick. Gemma wants to see what she's going to enjoy very soon."

Gemma touched Karlene's arm. "That's not nec..."

Frank's huge penis hung from his trouser flies. Gemma gasped at the size. Long thick and black.

"Touch it, darling, it's a monster. You'll feel that inside you, that's for sure."

Gemma poked a hand out. Her fingertips touched and she pulled them away as if it was red-hot.

Karlene took Gemma's fingers and wrapped them around the giant cock. "Frank does as he's told, don't you Frank?"

"Yes, Mistress Karlene." Frank's voice boomed baritone around the room bouncing off the windows.

"Good boy," said Karlene. "So, Pansy will have to tell Frank that she's a pansy princess with a little clitty and she can't satisfy his own wife, you Goddess Gemma. She will say Goddess Gemma deserves a real man. Therefore she, Pansy Princess understands Sir will have sex with Goddess Gemma. You, Gemma, will tell Pansy to say this while balancing in a low curtsey. She will have one leg behind the other, her pretty pink dress hanging over her smooth hairless legs. She will be blushing deeply, looking at the floor."

Gemma's eyes were wide like dinner plates, her mouth a perfect O. Her thumb stroked the huge penis lightly. Her face was a picture of astonishment.

"It's natural you, Gemma my dear, will fall in love with Frank, or at least his cock. You will send Pansy to stand outside behind your bedroom door. You will consummate your love while Pansy Princess waits behind the door listening to your love-making. She will hear your laughter and your breathing as it becomes heavier and heavier. The grunts of your boyfriend as he enters you. The noise of the bed as your love-making becomes more frantic in your passion. Then you'll cum together, both of you calling out and saying you love each other."

Gemma was breathing heavily at Karlene's words. "This is the final stage?" She looked at Frank's penis as it grew in her hand.

"Not quite, Gemma darling, we're part-way through the final stage of your training. You see, there are more duties a sissy cuckold has to perform."

Gemma's hand stroked Frank's erection now, her eyes half-closed. She put a hand in his trouser flies and pulled out Frank's huge balls. She cupped them, amazed at their size. She'd never seen anything this big before.

"Every time you make love to your hunky boyfriend Frank, you will call Pansy back into your master bedroom. Or maybe she is there watching. One of her cuckold duties is to clean up after you and Sir have finished making love. Pansy will clean you both with a perfumed cloth. Her job is to wipe away your boyfriend's sticky cum from between your legs and around your swollen labia. All the while, your boyfriend will be lying naked on top of the covers. His massive cock is now limp and expended, laying across one of his long massive thighs."

Gemma's eyes were closed, imaging the scene they would soon play out for real as her hand flowed to the end of Frank's cock and she pulled back his foreskin to reveal the largest gland she'd ever touched.

"Pansy must be made to clean Sir's limp penis, wiping away the last dribbles of his cum. I know you and your boyfriend will become aroused by this, by your power over Pansy."

Gemma gasped, her breathing getting faster and louder.

"I will arrange for one of my pretty sissies to join us. Lily will be perfect. I'll bring Lily into the bedroom. You will take Pansy and press her lips to Lily's. Do it gently, with care, with love. Your hands will be soft around Pansy's face, prodding pushing stroking. Open her mouth to lock onto Lily's lips like you did with her and Daisy earlier.

Pansy may not realise at first Lily is a sissy, not a real girl. I had a lot of work done on her. Pansy will find out though when she touches her clitty."

Karlene explained she will strip Lily down to her panties. Gemma, you will take Pansy's head again and push it down Lily's body. Press Pansy's lips pressed against Lily's small feminine body. You will bring Pansy's mouth to Lily's clitty through her panties. I'm sure she will pretend to fight against it but we'll hold her there and remove Lily's panties. We'll push Pansy's lips over your Lily's clitty and make her lick around her clitty head. It will be engorged, swollen, a drop of pre-cum sissy juice oozing from the end."

Gemma watched in astonishment

"Pansy's mouth will flow over Lily's enormous stiff clitty-cock. Pansy will take it in her mouth until she gags as it touches the back of her throat. Then she will move her mouth up to the end of Lily's erect clitty. Her lips will brush the end and her tongue will lap out against the end, licking. Gemma, you will guide Pansy's head back down over the strong firm clitty-cock again. Then pull Pansy up by her hair. Push her up and down, faster and faster, guiding Pansy by her hair. I'll be taking photos.

You will see Lily jerk and you will see her clitty cock pulsing cum deep into Pansy's mouth. You make Pansy swallow every drop. I sometimes find it useful to hold their noses. Pansy may have grey-white cum around her lips. You'll tell her to lick it away with her tongue and swallow every bit. Frank will watch and laugh. He enjoys that, don't you Frank?"

"Yes, Mistress Karlene," he boomed.

"Good boy," said Karlene.

"Karlene, you tell a great story. Will this happen though? I'm damp hearing your words, your descriptions.

"It's going to happen. Next week, Gemma."

"I don't think I can wait, Karlene." Gemma's eyes were part closed and she swayed on the sofa to the sound of an unheard tune.

"And now the pièce-de-resistance. Pansy is a girl. She has to be entered."

Gemma eagerly waited to hear.

15 — Recovery

"Lily will need a few minutes to recover, it's natural. She will have just shot a bucket load of cum into Pansy's mouth. We make Pansy help her by telling Pansy to stroke her clitty and giving it little sweet kisses. Make her kiss around and along the sides and on the end of it. I know Lily well, she recovers quickly, especially when another sissy is giving her clitty such tender sweet affection. You would never believe Lily used to be a macho businessman. She's now got a smaller waist and better tits than me."

Gemma listened as her breathing increased. She stroked Frank's cock faster, her hand gripped around it.

"You turn Pansy around and make her kneel on all fours on the bed. You guide her with your hands; be gentle. Your fingers will slide over Pansy's body, manoeuvring her into the position you want her. I find it works well when you take their clitty and use it like a joystick to put them where you want them. Then if they don't go where you want or they are too slow, you can squeeze their girly balls hard. Make her eyes water.

It works so much better this way since Pansy will feel your loving care and know you're doing it for her. She'll realise she's just a sissy princess who has to take clitties in her orifices. It's what she's there for."

Gemma's eyes were unblinking, concentrating on Karlene's every word. Frank groaned.

"Gemma, darling, why don't you have a suck on Frank and see what you'll be getting."

Gemma looked at the huge erection for a moment. It looked every inch of the eleven Karlene had told her. She put her mouth to the end gingerly. She looked back, a moment of doubt. She was about to suck another man's cock. The word *unfaithful* shot through her mind.

"It's what Pansy wants for you, darling."

Gemma wrapped her lips over the giant cock and pushed her mouth halfway down.

Karlene continued as Gemma sucked on the cock. "And you'll smear gel around Pansy's rear hole, your fingers wet and slimy moulding her little bum cheeks. You'll smear it around her sissy vagina, I'm sure by now she will be shaking with fear and anticipation. You'll push two fingers inside her, thick dollops of gel lining her insides, ready for the show.

You remove your fingers and, with one hand stroking Pansy's tiny clitty, you take your Lily's re-energised erection with your other hand. Your fingers grip around it and you guide it into Pansy's rear hole. Your hand slides to the small of Lily's back. You push against it and she moves forward and her erect clitty slides in to the hilt. She slaps against Pansy's bum cheeks. Pansy will feel full and she will be. I'll take more photos."

Gemma's head went faster over Frank's huge erection, her white face stark against his black cock.

"You guide Lily back and forth, in deep then back to the end, then thrust back in. Pansy might be complaining but ignore her. She's a sissy and she needs to be penetrated. You eventually see Lily start to orgasm. Your hand remains on her back so she cums strong and urgently into Pansy. A full eight inches deep.

You let Lily withdraw and lay back to recover. Her white cum oozes out from Pansy's tight hole in gloopy drops. You will have broken Pansy's sissy virginity. You tell sissy to thank your boyfriend for watching her have sex with Lily."

Frank groaned.

"Hold on dear, Frank's about to cum and it may be too much. I'll get Lily to take it for you this time." She clicked her fingers at Lily.

Gemma moved away and sat back, Karlene thought reluctantly. Lily replaced her at Frank's cock. Lily sucked expertly, up and down three times when Frank spurted into her sissy mouth. Again and again.

Lily choked for a moment, swallowed, and continued. It stopped. Lily licked around the end to remove that last of Frank's drops of cum and moved away.

Without missing a beat, Karlene continued. "By now, it will be time for Pansy to go to her pretty pink bedroom. She will sleep with Lily. I'll give you a little cock cage for Pansy. She mustn't be allowed to cum with Lily. They are sissies they are permanently hot for sissy clitty. When she's not performing for your and your boyfriend's entertainment, she will be locked up. You tell her to curtsey goodnight to Sir and to you, Goddess Gemma. Pansy might protest; she is desperate to cum. Out of love, you may need to slap her."

"Imagine this is your little Pansy. You slap her like this, darling." Karlene slapped Lily's cheek lightly several times. She pulled back and raised her hand. She pulled her arm back and slapped Lily's genitals.

"Now, Gemma darling, look at my face as I slap your pansy girl."

Gemma looked into Karlene's eyes with admiration for what she was learning.

"You tell Pansy how little femboys like her should be obedient, sweet princesses. They can no longer have sex with their sexy beautiful wives. Sex with a Goddess is only for Frank. Or other boyfriends."

Gemma nodded

"You pull Pansy to her bedroom by her clitty as she cries out and Lily will follow. You clamp your hand around her little girly balls. You make her bend over by her pretty girly bed as you spank her. You then kiss her on the cheek and tell her, *"There, there, pretty Pansy."*

You remove her little dress, shoes and socks and pull a short pink nightie over her head. It has the cartoon image of a blond-haired princess on it, with hair flowing down her back. I will join you and take more photos of Pansy. She'll be in her pretty nightie, her eyes red and watery from crying.

You tuck your little girl of a husband in bed with Lily and I will take some more photos of them cuddling and kissing. We'll tell them to kiss for a while. I then tell her with a hint of sternness she needs her beauty sleep. At the same time, you stroke her head and cheek lovingly. You wipe a tear away with one finger."

Gemma groaned at the image in her mind.

"We leave and I lock her bedroom door. We don't want her wandering around the house, she has to stay put while you have a hot, steamy long sex session with your new boyfriend. I know you will fall in love with him, it's inevitable, he's perfect for you. Your screams and groans will carry to little pansy princess's room where she weeps into the pillow, holding onto Lily.

You make love again with your boyfriend, delighting in the sensations of his enormous cock. You whisper in his ear, how adorable your sweet princess husband is and what a femboy she is. You'll adore having a real man with a real cock. Frank's a man who can finally satisfy you in the way your sissy husband never could. This is because she's a femboy sissy. Cute, adorable and sweet, but a little pansy who can't satisfy you.

Now Gemma, you are ready. Let's do this."

16 — The Power

The power to mould a man into the humiliated sissy he wanted to be was what life was about. It was life. Gemma had left Karlene's apartment a few minutes ago, looking different. Her cheeks glowed with a new vigour and she acted more assertive. She had slipped into the role of Sexy Goddess with ease. Karlene's new role as a Mistress tutor had begun.

It was a dark evening, the lesson had taken all day. Karlene stood by her picture window. Tall imposing glass and steel buildings lined the streets. Concrete bridges passed over the wide slow brown river was thronged with people and vehicles. She watched the river running through the centre of the city. The slow powerful tide moved to the sea, like the blood in her veins running to her heart. Powerful and unstoppable. The energy of the current coursed through her body.

Turning men into sissy princesses was her life, her reason for being. And soon it would be Paul Paige who was to become the next femboy. He had kept his sissiness locked up inside for too long. It was a façade she and his wife Gemma were about to break it down. Gemma was ready and it was time.

The lights of the city twinkled in the night like thousands of mini stars as a crescent moon rose through dark shadowy clouds. By this time next week, her plan would begin. Gemma will have the unsuspecting Pansy's new sissy bedroom decorated and furnished for a sissy princess.

Pansy Paul had no idea of the glorious fate about to befall him. Karlene had thought of Pansy as a sissy boy ever since college. And now Pansy's hot Goddess of a wife Gemma thought the same. Paul Paige, the former businessman, was to become Pansy, the sissy princess.

One week from now, Princess Pansy would start on the path to being a submissive pretty femboy in pretty dresses. Pansy would be obedient, speaking high and gentle, blushing and giggling like little girls do.

Karlene shivered at her thought. She wasn't cold, it was the power rush. It was better than an orgasm from being screwed by her 6ft 4in muscled boyfriend, Daniel and his eleven-inch cock. No, that wasn't right, she corrected herself. Daniel never screwed her; she screwed Daniel. Wasn't life great?

END OF SISSY HUSBAND 1

Don't miss out!

Visit the website below and you can sign up to receive emails whenever Lady Alexa publishes a new book. There's no charge and no obligation.

https://books2read.com/r/B-A-JTBM-MNOHE

BOOKS 2 READ

Connecting independent readers to independent writers.

Did you love *Sissy Husband 1*? Then you should read *Femboy Love 1*[1] by Lady Alexa!

[2]

Larry and Charlotte have been dating for six months and are in a loving relationship. They seem made for each other, sharing interests and having fun. Larry is besotted with Charlotte and would do anything for her. And Charlotte loves Larry because he is soft and gentle with no macho side.

He does have two tiny little problems. If she could fix them, all would be perfect.

He's rather small down below and unsatisfying sexually. She'd like him a little more delicate in his ways generally. It's time to make a few tweaks to Larry now they are a serious item.

---

1. https://books2read.com/u/mYl1oG

2. https://books2read.com/u/mYl1oG

If she could make him a little cuter, change a couple of areas in their unsatisfying love life, soften his appearance a little more and change his clothing to be prettier, things would be much improved. And she has a solution to his lack of size down-blow problem.

Everything is going to be perfect.

And Larry does say he'd do anything for her so she told him her problem.

This book describes scenes of a sexual nature including male to female gender transformation, sexual acts, forced feminisation, CFNM, humiliation and female domination. Strictly for adult readers aged 18+ only or the age of maturity in your region.

Read more at https://www.ladyalexauk.com.

Also by Lady Alexa

Becoming Joanne

Becoming Joanne 1

Becoming Joanne 2

Becoming Joanne 3

Femboy Love

Femboy Love 1

Feminized and Pretty

Feminized and Pretty 1

Feminized and Pretty 2

Feminized and Pretty 3

Feminized and Pretty 4

Forced Feminization

Forced Feminization Bundle 1

Lockdown Feminization
Lockdown Feminization 3
Lockdown Feminization 1

Sissy femboy transgender husband
Sissy Husband 2
Sissy Husband 3
Sissy Husband 1
Sissy Husband 4

Sissy Princess
Sissy Princess 2
Sissy Princess 1

Stepmother's Sissy
Stepmother's Sissy
Stepmother's Sissy 2
Stepmother's Sissy 3

Standalone
A Very Dominant Woman
Sissy Pink

Watch for more at https://www.ladyalexauk.com.

About the Author

I am an author and blogger on female led relationships, encouraged feminization and femdom and other erotica.

Read more at https://www.ladyalexauk.com.